DAUGHTERS
OF
TIME

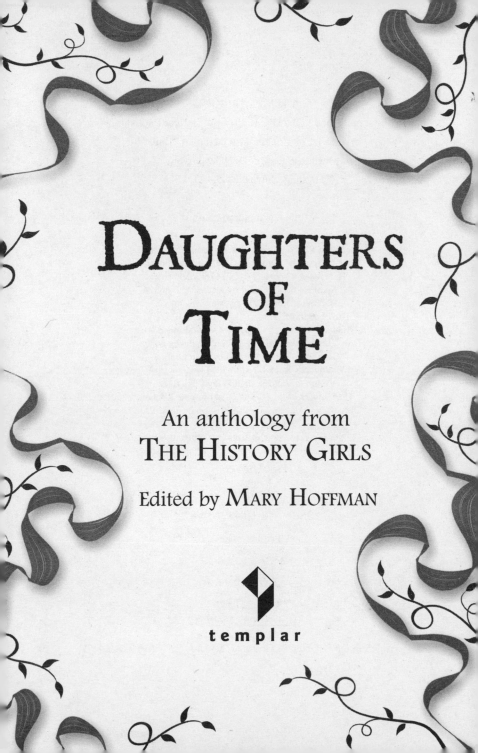

DAUGHTERS
OF
TIME

An anthology from
THE HISTORY GIRLS

Edited by MARY HOFFMAN

templar

A TEMPLAR BOOK

First published in the UK in 2014 by Templar Publishing,

an imprint of The Templar Company Limited,

Deepdene Lodge, Deepdene Avenue,

Dorking, Surrey, RH5 4AT, UK

www.templarco.co.uk

First UK edition

ISBN 978-1-84877-169-7

1 3 5 7 9 10 8 6 4 2

Printed in the UK by CPI Group (UK) Ltd, Croydon, CR0 4YY

In memory of Jan Mark,
writer and friend
(1943 - 2006)

'Truth is the daughter of time.'
Sir Francis Bacon

Introduction

HISTORY AT MY SCHOOL didn't feature many women. We learned about 'villeins', who I thought at first were evil creatures planning world domination. However, they turned out to be peasants in the Middle Ages – and they were all men. Then came more men, doing things like 'strip farming' and paying tithes to their feudal lords. And at the other end of the social scale, there were, of course, some kings.

I'm sure if I hadn't given up history at the age of fourteen, I would have at least been taught about Queen Elizabeth I and Queen Victoria, but I doubt whether, even now, students would come across many of the great women featured in this collection.

From the powerful resistance mounted by Queen Boudica and her fierce daughters, to the courageous protestors who demonstrated against nuclear missiles at Greenham Common, you will find plenty of characters to admire in this anthology.

They weren't all born to power; in fact, some of them came from very humble beginnings, but they have one thing in common – they were utterly dedicated to whatever their lives led them to do and be.

They were remarkable, but also in some ways completely ordinary, using their talents and gifts to make the very best of their lives, sometimes against tremendous odds.

They were pioneers – whether they were discovering truths about prehistoric life, healing soldiers in battle, flying planes, making their own choices about marriage, fighting for women's rights or just living a life of faith.

Thirteen authors of historical fiction have imagined what the lives of these inspiring women might have been like and have explained why the individual stories spoke to them.

We hope they will speak to you too.

MARY HOFFMAN

Contents

Tasca's Secret

A story about Queen Boudica
(c.30–c.60 AD)

BY KATHERINE ROBERTS

WHEN THE SOLDIERS CAME, Tasca had one foot on the shaft of the chariot and one hand twisted in her pony's mane. Her other hand clutched a spear, balanced overhead as her father had taught her before he died. Her mother thought Tasca too young to fight. Next time they quarrelled with a neighbouring tribe, Tasca would prove her wrong.

The ponies broke into a trot. Tasca took another step along the bouncing shaft.

"Steady!" she hissed at the pair. "This isn't easy, you know."

The pony harnessed on the other side – her sister's mare – snorted at the trees. The air rippled, as it did when the druids called on spirits. Then both ponies reared in terror as the forest exploded with men in leather armour brandishing swords.

Tasca swore as a branch knocked the spear out of her hand. She stumbled back along the chariot shaft and threw herself on to the platform, bruising her elbow. Anger filled her as the chariot careered out of control through the wood. She'd almost managed the trick all the best Iceni warriors used in battle – running along the shaft to surprise an enemy, before ducking back between the ponies for cover.

Then screams sounded in the village, and her anger turned to fear.

She gathered up the trailing reins, her heart thudding as she regained her balance and slowed the chariot. But before she could turn the ponies, a boy in a mud-splashed Roman tunic leapt into her path and flung himself at their bridles, dragging them to a stop.

"Don't go back there!" he warned.

Tasca scowled, recognising Marcus, the son of the local Roman governor. Her father, in his role as king of the Iceni, used to invite the boy's father to feasts in their roundhouse. Marcus would bring her little model horses, which he carved himself. Then the king had died and left half his lands to Tasca and her sister, and the governor had come no more. He did not feast with women, he said. This was the first time she'd seen her friend since her father's funeral, and she couldn't think what he was doing with the soldiers. The boy was no warrior.

"Marcus!" she said in relief. "Let go. I nearly ran you over."

But the boy clung on, white-faced. "No, Tasca, I'm serious. Father sent those men here. I came as fast as I could to warn you. They've orders to teach your mother a lesson."

She frowned. "What sort of lesson?" Then she smelled smoke and heard more screams. "They're burning our village!"

"They'll do worse if you try to help. Quick, someone's coming... hide!" Marcus grabbed her long braid, pulling her off the platform and into the bushes. The ponies bolted with the empty chariot bouncing behind them.

Some soldiers ran past, dragging a girl with copper hair between them. The golden torc of a princess gleamed around her neck. Her wrists had been bound, but she was fighting her captors like a true Iceni warrior. "Camorra!" Tasca yelled, realising the captive was her sister.

Marcus put his hand over her mouth. "Shh," he hissed. "You can't help her now, or those men will catch you, too. Come with me. You'll be safe in my father's house – put this on." He pulled a ragged dress out of the bag he was carrying.

Tasca stared at the dress. It was filthy and smelled of somebody else's sweat. "I'm not wearing that—" Her words ended in a splutter as Marcus scooped up some mud and smeared it across her mouth.

He smiled grimly at her expression. "No one'll recognise you now. Keep your head down. I'll smuggle you in the back gate of our camp. It's the last place they'll look for you."

As they travelled through the forest, Tasca worried about her family. She whistled for her ponies, worried about them too. But only the wind replied, moaning though the trees like druid horns. She shuddered and hurried to catch up with her friend.

The Roman camp was more organised than their village. It had huts arranged in a grid, a big house for the governor, and a ditch all around with stakes driven into the ground to keep enemies and wild animals out. And keep the British slaves in.

Two nights passed. Marcus showed Tasca where she could sleep, and smuggled her food from his father's table. She discovered she could wander freely around the camp, as long as she stayed inside the stakes. She passed the time gathering useful leaves and roots, which she slipped into an old pouch she'd found.

Wounded men began to limp out of the woods. Some were carried in on stretchers and taken to the blood tent, where doctors worked to heal the injured. Tasca crept in after them to find out what had happened to her people.

While she hesitated at the tent flap, a soldier called out to her: "You, girl! Bring me water!"

Tasca scowled. She opened her mouth to protest that she wasn't a slave. Then, remembering her disguise, she ducked her head and picked up the water jug.

The wounded soldier spat. "Told you a whipping wouldn't stop the crazy woman, didn't I?" he grumbled to his friends. "Now she's roused the Trinovantes against us! We should've crucified the druid-lover and her wildcat of a daughter while we had the chance, instead of letting them run off to wail to the other tribes about what we did to them. Mars only knows where the other girl got to."

Tasca clenched her fist and wished she still had her spear. She poured water into a bowl and carefully added a few crushed leaves from her pouch. She took the soldier his water. The wounded man snatched it from her and drank deeply.

"Taste good, Roman?" Tasca whispered in Latin. "That's for what you just called my mother and sister."

He looked up in surprise. His eyes widened as he realised who she must be. Then he died.

That evening, Tasca pushed past the guards at the door and marched into the governor's house. She found Marcus reclining on a couch beside his father, eating grapes and cheese from a low table. The governor wore a toga and was using his dagger to eat. He frowned at Tasca.

"I'm not one of your slaves!" she said, glaring at

her friend. "I'm a princess of the Iceni. And I want to go home now."

Marcus sat up with a start. He shook his head urgently at her. One of the guards stepped forward, but the governor raised a hand. He swung his feet to the floor and looked Tasca in the eye. He did not seem surprised by her announcement, and a little chill went down her back.

"It's just a story to keep you safe," the governor said, glancing at Marcus, who avoided Tasca's gaze. "Words can't hurt you, can they?"

"But your men are talking about crucifying my mother and sister!" Tasca said.

"Small chance of that," muttered the governor, looking thoughtfully at her. "The queen must know we have you by now, yet she refuses to stop fighting. Perhaps she needs more encouragement. Come here."

He picked up his dagger and wiped it clean on his leg. Marcus paled.

Tasca stiffened and looked over her shoulder. The guards stood right behind her, ready to catch her if she tried to run. She shouldn't have burst in here like this. She should have climbed the fence and run away into the woods…

The governor laughed. "I'm not going to kill you, silly girl! I could have done that a hundred times already, while you slept under my roof. I just want some of that bright hair."

He lifted her braid and sliced it off. He passed the coil of copper hair to one of his men and muttered an order.

Tasca shook her head, which felt strangely light.

"Don't look at me like that," the governor said. "They'll give it to your mother with a message from me, and then maybe she'll see sense and give herself up. You can't go back to your village anyway – it's not there any more. The queen of the Iceni is on the road with her army, burning cities and terrorising decent, law-abiding people. She's got to be stopped."

Tasca glared at Marcus. "You brought me here to be your hostage, didn't you? I hate you!"

"I saved your life," Marcus mumbled, his dark eyes full of pain.

"I'll kill you if you hurt my mother and sister."

The governor sighed. "That's exactly what the queen said about you, so we'd better make sure you stay alive, hadn't we?"

To find out what was happening outside the camp, Tasca took water to the wounded. If they were kind to her, she used her knowledge of herbs to ease their pain. If they were rude about her family, they died.

She discovered that her mother had burned the towns of Camulodunum and Londinium. Some said the Iceni queen had ten thousand warriors, others claimed a hundred thousand. The Romans were panicking and calling their legions back from the druid stronghold of Mona. The countryside was full of refugees, smoke and rumours.

In her dreams, Tasca caught glimpses of battle and blood, and began to worry about her ponies again. Had her mother used them to pull a chariot in battle? They would be frightened and bolt, and then the queen would get angry and whip them. She should never have let Marcus talk her into leaving them behind.

Towards the end of summer, a messenger arrived on a sweaty horse. "Where's the governor?" he yelled. "I bring a message from Suetonius Paullinus! He's got a plan to finish the demon queen, once and for all."

Tasca turned cold. She followed the messenger into the governor's house and listened at the door, but could hear nothing. Then the door opened and Marcus rushed out, almost knocking her over.

"You've got to warn your mother!" he hissed, grabbing her wrist and dragging her outside. "They're going to set an ambush. If she brings her army along Watling Street, everyone's going to die, my people as well as yours. Take my dagger and go – you're the only one who can stop her."

Tasca stared at the weapon. "If this is another trick…"

"It's not a trick!" His anguished look told her he spoke the truth. "Please go, Tasca. You were right, before. Father wants to use you as bait for the trap, and I couldn't bear it if you got hurt." He slipped the dagger into her belt and pushed her towards the fence.

Tasca didn't need to be told twice. While Marcus distracted the sentries, she darkened her cheeks with mud and crawled along the ditch until she'd passed the final guard. Then she squeezed through the stakes and ran into the forest, hiding herself between the roots of a tree.

They came after her, of course. Soldiers prodded the leaves so close to her hand that a spear grazed her fingers. She kept very still, biting her lip so she wouldn't cry out. When they had gone, she bound the wound with a rag torn from the hem of her dress. Then she took the secret paths deep into the forest, until she found the druid grove where her mother worshipped the goddess.

She climbed the sacred oak, blew the horn that hung in its branches, and waited.

Tasca spent three uncomfortable nights up the ancient tree, wondering if any of her people were left alive to hear the call of the horn. Once a troop of Roman soldiers ran underneath, boasting about what they would do to the Iceni queen once they captured her. With only the mistletoe to hide her,

Tasca broke into a sweat. But the goddess must have been protecting her, because they did not look up and see her. She dozed off again. Then she heard a familiar snort below, and jerked awake.

She looked down. A chariot had entered the grove, drawn by a pair of limping ponies. One of them raised its head and whickered. Tasca slid stiffly down the tree and hugged her pony. "Poor thing," she whispered. "What has Mother done to you?"

The pony blew into her shorn hair, while the driver of the chariot stared coldly down at her. It was her sister Camorra.

"Had enough of your Roman friends, then?" she asked.

"I came to warn you!" Tasca blurted out. "They're setting an ambush. They've got a legion, at least. You mustn't go any further—"

"Bring her here," a woman called from the edge of the trees.

Tasca shivered. She barely recognised her mother. The queen's grey-streaked hair had been braided with human bones. Her arms and cheeks were painted with blue spirals. Roman heads, buzzing with flies and crusted with blood, hung from the shaft of her chariot. Tasca felt the chill of the queen's gaze as two Iceni warriors rushed to catch her arms.

"Let go of me," she said. "I'm not running away. I came to find you. A Roman legion is waiting to ambush you!"

"Good," said the queen. "Show us where, and I'll add a thousand Roman heads to my chariot shaft."

"But you can't fight them," Tasca said. "Don't you understand? It's an ambush! They've been planning it for months. You must turn back."

"Not another word!" the queen said, her expression furious. "We outnumber them ten to one. You can ride with your sister, and when we've defeated these Romans maybe I'll let you help me take revenge for what they did to us. We'll see how tough they are, when I hold their governor's child helpless in my camp."

The warriors lifted Tasca into the chariot, and Camorra whipped the ponies into a gallop. Tasca tried to protest that they were lame, but her sister did not seem to hear.

They came upon the Roman army at dawn. The legion waited in a glittering line at the edge of the wood, above where the road passed through a narrow valley. The Iceni army was strung out as far as the river. A line of carts carrying small children and supplies rumbled along at the back.

A shiver went down Tasca's spine. The Romans stood eerily silent, their big shields joined together like a wall and their swords pointing through the gaps. Her mother's army, in contrast, yelled and whooped defiantly, while the druids blew their horns to call on the favour of the goddess. Some young Trinovante warriors, caught up in the battle fever, raced up the slope to attack the Roman line, but died on the sharp swords.

The Roman general, Suetonius Paullinus, sat his big black horse at the top of the hill, directing his men. The queen pointed to him and yelled, "My best stallion and a chariot of gold for the warrior who brings me that man's head!"

The horns blew. The army whooped its delight at the challenge. "Boudica!" yelled ten thousand throats. "Queen Boudica for victory!" Men and women brandished their weapons and rushed the Roman line. The Romans pressed forwards down the slope, and people began to scream and die.

Tasca huddled in the chariot, sickened by the blood, as Camorra drove up the hill. Thankfully, the ponies were too lame to keep up with the charge. Her mother's chariot thundered past them, the queen yelling encouragement and brandishing her spear. Camorra shouted at Tasca to take the reins and leapt for the back of the queen's chariot. But she missed her footing and clung on with one hand, hanging dangerously over the edge.

"Camorra!" Tasca cried, seeing a Roman soldier grab her sister's ankle.

The ponies had no speed left. She had only one chance of reaching Camorra in time.

Tasca ran along the shaft and kicked the Roman's wrist as hard as she could. He yelled in pain as the bone broke, releasing Camorra. Tasca ducked back between the ponies for cover and left the confused man blinking at the queen's chariot, where Camorra had regained her feet and was brandishing her sword triumphantly. By the time he realised the trick, Tasca had turned her chariot and was racing back down the hill.

She steered the ponies to the riverbank, where it was quieter. But she couldn't block out the screams. She watched in horror as the Romans threw wave after wave of javelins to kill her mother's warriors, and then came running down the hill to slaughter those who had retreated to protect the carts. She couldn't see where her mother and sister had gone. But Suetonius Paullinus still sat on his horse at the top of the hill, head intact.

Tasca hardly cared that she had managed the famous Iceni chariot trick. She didn't even want to know who was winning. She jumped out of the chariot and buried her face in her pony's sweaty mane until it was over.

When the sun had turned the river to blood, Camorra returned and touched her on her shoulder.

"Tasca?" she said gently. "Come. Mother's asking for you."

Tasca raised her tear-streaked face. "She's still alive?"

Camorra hesitated. "Yes. She took a wound but she'll be fine. I killed the Roman who wounded her. I didn't know you'd learned Father's chariot trick. Thank you for helping me back there."

"Did we win?"

Her sister's expression told her otherwise. "The Trinovantes deserted, and Suetonius's men went after them. Our army's finished. But we captured the governor's boy, so we've still got some bargaining power. They're in the druid grove. This way."

Tasca's mouth dried with fear for her friend. *Marcus*, she thought.

The trees around the druid grove were hung with bones, which rattled as they passed. The ponies refused to enter. Tasca shuddered as she dismounted from the chariot, sure she could hear the spirits of the dead warriors wailing.

In the clearing the queen leaned on a spear staring at her captive. The boy knelt in a puddle of blood, his arms bound tightly behind him and his head bowed. A druid with a ceremonial scythe stood beside him. Tasca's breath caught, but the blood did not seem to belong to her friend.

The queen looked round impatiently. "Ah, here she is! Daughter, I promised you could take your revenge. Blood your dagger and cut off this Roman whelp's ears for me. We'll send them back to his father with a message, like he sent me your beautiful hair."

"But that was only my hair—" Tasca protested.

Marcus' dark gaze silenced her. "Do it," he whispered through chattering teeth. "Or your people will never follow you when you're queen."

Tasca shook her head. "Don't be silly, I'm not going to be queen. I'll help you escape." She took a quick breath, and used the dagger to cut Marcus's bonds. He just knelt there, shivering and staring at her. "Run!" she hissed. "Your father's people are only over that hill. You won the battle, don't you understand?"

The queen's eyes flashed in anger. She took a step towards Tasca and grabbed her wrist to seize the dagger. Then she let out a moan and staggered.

"Mother!" Camorra ran to catch the queen as she collapsed. The druid lowered his scythe and blew a mournful note on his horn. "The goddess has spoken," he said. "The boy shall not die today. She will take another to her realm." People stared around in fear as the bones in the trees rattled again.

In the confusion, Marcus finally fled.

They carried the queen to what remained of the Iceni camp. Camorra tried to follow, but Tasca pushed her away and told her to help the druid with the other wounded.

"I'll tend our mother," she told her sister firmly. "I know herbs. Bring me that old pouch I was wearing when you found me."

By the light of the moon, she collected water from the river and added the last of the leaves from the slave-pouch. She carried the bowl to her mother's bedside and held her head while she drank.

"The Roman boy had better be worth it, daughter," the queen whispered as the potion took effect. Then her eyes closed, and silent tears ran down Tasca's cheeks.

Queen Boudica died peacefully in her sleep that night.

In the morning, Tasca and Camorra hung charms from the bridles of their ponies and led the queen's chariot bearing her body through the camp. The Iceni wept, of course, but a sense of relief hung over the survivors. The fighting was over at last. The Romans would restore order to their towns, and the farmers could once more grow crops without fear of losing them to Boudica's army.

Marcus and his father were waiting for them at the bridge.

"You realise your lands belong to the emperor now, don't you?" said the governor, helping his son into their chariot. "If you resist again, I won't be able to help you a second time."

Camorra scowled, but Tasca put a hand on her sister's arm. "We know."

"Suetonius Paullinus will be back before nightfall," the governor continued. "You should have half a day's start if you head for the forest. I'll tell him we couldn't find your bodies. The emperor needn't know the truth of what happened here today."

His gaze rested on Tasca as he said this, and she wondered if he had guessed how some of the wounded men in his camp had died while she had been his slave.

When, a few years later, she and Marcus had daughters of their own, Tasca showed them how to run along a chariot shaft to trick their enemies, and how to blow a druid's horn to summon help if they needed it. But she did not teach them which leaf from the forest will steal a person's spirit quietly in the night.

Some secrets are best left untold.

Why I Chose Queen Boudica

I chose this story because I enjoy writing battle scenes, especially when the warriors are girls! And it's the right period of history for me to include a few horses, which always seem to find their way into my books. With the druids involved, I even managed to include a tiny bit of magic (but don't tell my editor).

KATHERINE ROBERTS

Queen Boudica Facts

Queen Boudica (sometimes called Boudicca or Boadicea) was a Celtic queen of the Iceni tribe, also known as 'the people of the horse'. Her name means 'victory'.

Around 60 AD she led a revolt against the Romans, who had tried to seize the Iceni lands and wealth after her husband, King Prasutagus, died.

Boudica had two daughters, whose names are not known. I've called them Tasca and Camorra in this story because these names are currently in popular use, although they are almost certainly fictional.

After burning the cities of *Camulodunum* (Colchester), *Londinium* (London) and *Verulamium* (St Albans), Queen Boudica's rebels were finally defeated by a much smaller Roman army at the Battle of Watling Street.

Boudica died after the battle, but nobody knows how. She might have taken poison rather than be captured by the Romans, or she might have been badly wounded in the fighting and died later.

Her body was never found.

Nobody knows what happened to her two daughters.

The Lady of the Mercians

A story about Aethelflaed
(c.870–918)

BY SUE PURKISS

EDWARD SHOVED HIS SWORD into its scabbard and glared at his sister. Did she have to win every single time?

"It's not fair," he complained. "You're a girl. You shouldn't be so good with a sword."

"Oh?" said Flaeda, inspecting her blade and polishing off a speck of dirt with her sleeve. "So what should I be good at?"

Edward thought about it. What did other boys' sisters do? "Weaving," he suggested. "Or needlework. You could make a tapestry." His eyes lit up as he warmed to the idea. "You could do one of me fighting!"

Flaeda laughed. "But you haven't done any fighting yet – not proper fighting, anyway."

"I'll do some soon!" he said. He was thirteen, and growing fast. "You're only two years older than me. Soon *I'll* be riding out with Father while you're at home with Mother."

Light flashed from Flaeda's blade as it arced through the air, ending up with the point pressed just under his chin.

"Ow!" he complained. "That hurts!"

Flaeda kept the tip of her sword exactly where it was. "Then don't say such ridiculous things. My place is beside Father. Just as it was at Athelney, and just as it always will be."

Edward pushed the sword aside, scowling. It still rankled that at the time of the kingdom's greatest danger, he'd been packed off into safety with his mother and his little sisters. It was Flaeda who'd been by their father's side when King Alfred had emerged from his hiding place in the marshes round Athelney to win a glorious victory against Guthrum and his army of Vikings at the Battle of Edington: Flaeda who'd had all the fun.

"You were only nine," he said. "You didn't fight."

"No," said Flaeda, sheathing her sword. "I didn't fight. But I was there."

She could remember the battle so well: the flash of spears, the clash of swords, the battle cries, the screams, the black crows circling greedily overhead. The thought of the screams and the crows made her shiver still. But she also remembered the great roar that rose from the throats of the men of Wessex when Guthrum and his Vikings turned tail and ran away. Victory was sweet. She hadn't lost the taste for it.

"Flaeda!" Her mother was walking towards them through the orchard which separated the great hall from the practice ground. Queen Eahlswith broke off a spray of blossom and held it to her face, breathing in its scent. "The first flowers of spring are such a delight," she said, smiling. "Edward, I believe Rathgar is looking for you. Something about your hawk... Something you neglected to do?" Edward groaned, and ran off to find the old falconer.

Then Eahlswith turned to Flaeda. "Come," she said, her dark eyes suddenly serious. "Let us sit on this bench. It is pleasant here in the sunshine, is it not?" Flaeda felt a twinge of alarm. She was often in trouble: for spending too much time in the stables or the smithy, for being untidy and unladylike, for neglecting her weaving. But she sensed that this was about something different.

"What is it, Mother?" she asked anxiously. "Tell me, please."

And Eahlswith told her.

Flaeda leapt to her feet. Her eyes were filled with horror and an angry flush stained her cheeks. "MARRIED? To Aethelred? But he's *old*! And he lives in *Mercia*!"

"Of course he lives in Mercia," said Eahlswith. "He's the lord of the Mercians – where else would he live? It's a very nice place – it was my home before I married your father. You know that. Really, Flaeda…"

"I'm going to see Father. He won't let this happen. He needs me. I—"

She whirled round and raced towards the hall. How could they think of such a thing? She had to find her father. She'd talk to him, and he'd understand, and then everything would be all right again…

King Alfred was at his table, writing. As Flaeda burst in, he sighed, and laid down his quill.

"So. Your mother has spoken to you."

She stopped, suddenly uncertain. So he knew… but of course he knew. How could he not?

Marriage to the lord of the Mercians was not a scheme her mother would have cooked up all by herself. Still, she could make him understand – she must!

But in the end, as she met his steady gaze, she could only stammer: "Why, Father – why?"

"Oh, Flaeda, think. Surely I've taught you to do that? By this marriage, Mercia will be bound even more closely to Wessex. Then how shall the Northmen stand against the two kingdoms together?" His eyes blazed. "You know my dream, Flaeda. One day, all the Saxon kingdoms will be united – under the rule of the House of Wessex! Think of that, Flaeda – think of *that*! This is a necessary step."

She pressed her hands to her temples. Dreams – always dreams! What about *her* life? What about *her* dreams? "He's an old man!" she burst out.

He raised his eyebrows. "Am *I* an old man?"

"No, no, of course not, but…"

"Well then. Aethelred is younger than me. Besides, you've met him. He came here just after he became the lord of the Mercians, a couple of years after Edington. You talked to him, you liked him. And he said you had the cleverest head he'd ever come across on such young shoulders."

She had a vague memory of someone tall, someone who'd listened as she explained her father's plans to build a series of *burhs* – fortified towns with strong walls, where the people could take shelter in times of danger. She'd enjoyed the attention, she remembered; he had made her feel important.

"I don't want to go away," she whispered. "I don't want to leave here. I don't want to leave you. You – you *need* me."

He rose from his chair, walked over to her, held out his arms.

"I *do* need you," he said. "But, my dearest girl, not here. I need you to be my eyes and ears in Mercia. You will always be part of this family, Flaeda, always part of Wessex. But half of you is Mercian already – don't forget that. You can weave our two countries together in a way that no one else can. Come now – will you help me, as you have always done?"

How could she refuse? She hugged him. But then she stepped back, her hands at her sides, her shoulders straight. "I had better not be called Flaeda any more," she said clearly. "That's a little girl's name. My proper name is Aethelflaed. That's what everyone must call me from now on."

And gathering all her dignity about her, she left the room.

Two weeks later, it was time for Aethelflaed and her company to leave for Gloucester, where Aethelred, her future husband, was to meet her. All being well, the journey would take four or five days. They would spend the nights under the stars.

As the road climbed up out of Winchester, Aethelflaed reined in her horse and turned to look down at the city for one last time. Her family was seldom in one place for long, but Winchester was the capital of Wessex; if anywhere was home, this was. She gazed at the hall, and the fine stone minster which was being built close by it. Houses and workshops lined the streets, newly laid out according to Alfred's design. She sighed. If only some of her family could have travelled with her! But she understood – in these dangerous times it was foolish to travel unless there was no help for it.

Still, she knew all the men who were riding with her. A few of them, like Osric, who was leading the party, had been at Athelney with her – brothers in arms. Her maidservant, Estrid, also rode by her side. The girl looked terrified, and they had only just left home. "What's the matter, Estrid?" Aethelflaed teased. "Do you think there are raiders waiting to pounce on us?"

"There might be," retorted Estrid, "and then what should we do?"

"Why," said Aethelflaed, "we'd fight them. What else? But don't worry – we shan't see any so close to Winchester. They're not that stupid."

Suddenly, she realised that Osric was awaiting her orders. The whole procession had stopped when she had, and without her say-so, they would not move on. She was in charge. She pulled on the reins, turned resolutely away from home, and leaned forward to pat her horse's neck. It felt warm, a little rough. The horse snickered in appreciation. "We have a long way to go," she said. "We had best press on."

Osric nodded in approval. "North-west then. To Mercia!"

Travelling over the downs, across Wiltshire, they made good time. Aethelflaed loved this country. It reminded her of the ride to Athelney all those years ago. It had been winter when Guthrum and his Viking army had attacked Chippenham. Alfred had been there for Christmas. They had been taken by surprise – no one, after all, fought in the depths of winter. Knowing that he was the one Guthrum was after, Alfred had sent his family south to safety in Winchester, while he himself rode west with just a small band of men to hide in the marshes. He had hunted there as a boy; he knew the secret ways. He knew he would be safe there.

Aethelflaed smiled as she remembered how she had tricked her way into Alfred's company by dressing as a boy. How angry her father had been when he discovered her! Now she was wearing boy's clothes again. To her mother's disgust, she had insisted on it, pointing out how much more practical a tunic and leggings would be for the journey.

Snow had covered the low, curving hills then. Now, in May, the springy turf was starred with violets and cowslips. Kestrels kept their balance with swiftly beating wings, and buzzards soared high up in the blue sky. Aethelflaed shook her dark gold hair free and laughed in delight as she set her horse to a gallop – there was nowhere to hide in this open country, so the danger from raiders was slight.

Four days later, as they drew closer to Gloucester, the lie of the land was very different. The smooth sweep of the downs had given way to secretive wooded valleys and twisting paths. The company fell silent, and Osric sent scouts out ahead. Estrid's eyes darted from side to side; even the wind rustling in the leaves made her jump nervously.

"Ride behind me," said Aethelflaed. "You're making me twitchy!"

"I don't like these woods," muttered Estrid. "There could be anything hiding in them – goblins! Or wolves. Or outlaws!"

"If those were all we had to worry about," said Osric, "I should be well pleased."

Just as Aethelflaed opened her mouth to answer, she was startled by the sound of a horse crashing through the trees. Osric immediately moved his horse in front of her, drawing his scramasax from his belt as he did so. But it was only one of the scouts.

"It's just Acwald," Osric said in relief.

But the scout was sitting at a peculiar angle, leaning to one side. Aethelflaed gasped – one of his sleeves was soaked in blood.

"Raiders!" Acwald groaned as he slid from the saddle. "Close behind…"

"Fool!" snapped Osric. "He'll have led them straight to us."

Aethelflaed could hear no sound of pursuers. "He rode swiftly. He meant to warn us, and he did."

"Even so, they'll be here soon," said Osric.

He grasped Aethelflaed's reins. "My lady, you must take shelter. Go deeper into the wood while we deal with them."

Indignantly, Aethelflaed snatched the reins back. "I'll do no such thing!" She scanned the area, her sharp eyes missing nothing. "There! That trench, just where the ground begins to rise. There's room for all of us in there. Get Estrid and the horses out of the way, and then we can surprise them. It'll give us the advantage. Estrid – take care of Acwald."

Aethelflaed was her father's daughter, and she was not to be disobeyed.

As the raiders rode into the clearing a few minutes later, they saw a mass of hoofprints leading off the path deeper into the wood. Their leader, a stocky man with shoulders almost as broad as he was tall, smiled in satisfaction. At a signal from him, they all dismounted, ready to follow the tracks into the trees.

Aethelflaed crouched silently in the trench with Osric and the others, her sword at the ready, perfectly still. Timing was everything. When the raiders had their attention firmly focused in the wrong direction – then they would swoop.

It worked perfectly. The raiders fought fiercely, but the Saxons made the most of the advantage surprise had given them. Aethelflaed's sword sang; she was everywhere, darting and stinging like an angry wasp, her hair flying loose.

As yet another Viking fell, she paused to look round. To her horror, she saw the bulky shape of the raiders' leader, arms raised, battleaxe clutched in both raised hands, poised in front of Osric, who had fallen to his knees. The chieftain was about to deal the death blow. Yelling, she leapt in front of him. In his eyes she saw first surprise, then a glint of satisfaction – *she* was the one he wanted.

"You want to fight me?" he roared. "With *that* pretty plaything?"

She leapt in under his guard. The startled look on his face was almost comical as the pretty plaything drove in between his ribs.

"My lady!" gasped Osric.

She tugged her sword out of the raider's body.

Then she helped Osric to his feet and looked round. It was over. The raiders were either dead, wounded, or fleeing. Suddenly, Aethelflaed began to feel shaky. She had never killed anyone before. She pushed the tip of her sword into the ground and leaned on it. She must be strong…

Then the ground was pounding with the sound of more hoofbeats. "Oh, no!" she groaned. "Not more of them!"

But the band of warriors that now galloped into the clearing was led by a tall man, a Saxon, who leapt from his horse and strode over to her, his hands held out in greeting. Just as her head began to swim and her knees to buckle, she realised that there was something familiar about him.

A little later she opened her eyes. "We won, didn't we?" she whispered.

The tall man smiled. "My lady, from what I hear of all that has happened here, I think you will always win."

"Are you…?"

"I am Aethelred." He took her hands and

pulled her to her feet. "And I bid you welcome to Mercia!"

In less than an hour they arrived at Gloucester. In the centre, on a rise where the great hall stood, she looked round in silence. The Mercians and her own escort waited. She could see that this had once been a fine town. But the walls had been breached, and many of the buildings were in ruins. "Guthrum," said Aethelred, following her gaze, "before your father humbled him. Before the last king left to seek shelter in Rome." He looked at her. "But I shall rebuild it. *We* shall rebuild it. This town will one day be as safe and strong as all those *burhs* you once told me about."

His eyes were bright and blue, she saw, and they shone with energy and passion. "There is much to do. Will you help me? Will you be my Lady of the Mercians?"

Aethelflaed smiled and held out her hands. "I will," she said.

And all around them their people raised a great cheer.

Why I Chose Aethelflaed

I became fascinated by Aethelflaed (pronounced 'Athelfleed') when I wrote *Warrior King*, which finished with the victory of her father, Alfred the Great, over the Vikings at the Battle of Edington. I was delighted to discover her, because I needed a child's viewpoint and, at ten or thereabouts, she was the perfect age. I was also interested to find out that in later life, after her husband's death, the people of Mercia chose her to be the leader. And she wasn't a leader in name only – she led them into battle and became known as *Myrcna Hlaefdige* – the lady of the Mercians. In the *Annals of Ulster*, she was described at her death as '*famosissima regina Saxonum*' – the most famous queen of the Saxons. Those same annals ignored the passing of her brother, King Edward, and even that of her great father, King Alfred.

So, I was delighted to have the opportunity to take up her story again. Few individual women emerge from the Dark Ages – I think Aethelflaed should be better known.

SUE PURKISS

Aethelflaed Facts

Aethelflaed was the eldest of Alfred the Great's children, born in approximately 870.

She married Aethelred, Lord of Mercia, in 886. On her journey to the wedding, her company is said to have been attacked by a raiding party. Legend has it that she coordinated the fight back. I have not been able to find a source from the time to confirm that this happened, but then, written records from this time are few and far between.

In 911, Aethelred died, and the people chose Aethelflaed to be their ruler. Her husband had been seriously ill for at least ten years before this, and she had ruled in his place for this time. She fought many campaigns, often with her brother, Edward, who had succeeded their father as King of Wessex.

Aethelflaed fostered her brother's eldest son, Athelstan, who later became king in his turn. It was a common custom for the sons of noblemen to be fostered in the household of a trusted friend or relative. However, it's also true that Edward's wife was not Athelstan's mother, so perhaps this played a part in the decision to send him to be fostered away from Edward's court.

Aethelflaed died in 918.

Her daughter, Aelfwyn, then ruled Mercia very briefly before Edward removed her from the throne and took her into Wessex. Perhaps Edward thought that the Mercians might rally behind Aelfwyn, which would have got in the way of his ultimate aim – for the House of Wessex to rule all England. Or perhaps he thought she wasn't strong enough to lead the Mercians in those troubled times. Whatever the reason, nothing is heard of Aelfwyn after this.

The Queen's Treasure

*A story about Eleanor of Aquitaine
(c.1122–1204)*

BY ADÈLE GERAS

WAKING FELT LIKE COMING UP and up through dark water. Juana looked around the unfamiliar room – high ceiling, narrow window, hard wooden chair at the foot of the bed – and struggled, through the fog that filled her head, to remember where she was. It wasn't home.

The door opened and a woman dressed in pale grey garments came and stood beside her and took her hand. A nun – of course. They were in a convent. Juana was beginning to remember everything. As her memories returned, she was overcome with homesickness. Her head ached and there were tears filling her eyes. Even though she tried to stop them, they wouldn't be contained and spilled on to her cheeks.

"Don't cry, child," said the nun. "You are come to your true senses and awake, and for that we must give thanks to God. Soon, in a few days, you'll be ready to continue on your travels. I'm sure you're longing for that. You're very young… how young exactly?"

"Almost twelve years old, Sister," whispered Juana, and was relieved to discover that she still had a voice and could recall her age.

"The young find bed rest very boring," the nun continued. "Or so I have heard. My old bones, on the other hand, would be grateful for a good long lie-down." The nun, whose face was as wrinkled as a walnut between the folds of her headdress, smiled and wiped Juana's cheeks with a kerchief taken from under the edge of her sleeve.

Her 'travels'… Juana wished fervently that she'd never been picked to go on this horrible journey. She'd never asked to accompany Queen Eleanor and the Princess Berengaria to Italy. She'd never said she wanted to be jolted and tossed on wagons over every sort of road, through mud and rain and up hills and down rivers on hired barges, just so that the Old Queen could arrange a marriage for her son, Richard. But now, in the year of our Lord 1191, he was the king of England, and known everywhere as the Lionheart. Even Juana could see that for the princess of a country like Navarre to become queen of England was something of a miracle and an opportunity not to be missed.

When the call came, Juana's mother had been

happy and proud. "You'll have adventures," she said, clasping her hands together in delight then hugging Juana to her bosom. "Such adventures as I could never dream of. And see such sights! High towers, rich palaces, fine houses full of grand ladies and gentlemen. Knights, even kings."

"But how do you know what it'll be like?" Juana had said. "You've never travelled. And I can see towers and palaces and kings here, too. Isn't King Sancho a king? Is Navarre not a kingdom? Don't we have knights?"

"Of course. Not only is it a kingdom but we, too, love music and song and poetry just like the people of Aquitaine. That was where Queen Eleanor lived when she was a young girl. Then her father died and she was packed off to marry Louis of France so as to form an alliance between the lands that each of them ruled. She wasn't much older than you when that happened, you know. So yes, we're a kingdom, but compared with England and France, our little corner of the world is nothing much to speak of. And how good of Princess Berengaria to choose you of all the

maids to travel with her and Queen Eleanor...
It's an honour."

Queen Eleanor of Aquitaine. She was the one
who'd ridden ahead to the convent when Juana fell
ill and persuaded the Mother Superior to take in
every one of the travelling party and shelter them
for days. The Old Queen, as she was known, was
fearless and clever and determined to have her
own way in everything. She was the one keenest
to climb mountains and cross fields and rivers
and risk illness and danger and discomfort. She
was the one with a sharp and clever tongue and
an even sharper eye for spying opportunities and
difficulties and moreover, she knew how to deal
with any problem that came her way. But she was
nearly seventy years old, too, and there were times
when Princess Berengaria or one of the guards
tried to get her to slow down.

Whenever they did so, Eleanor gave them the
rough side of her tongue. "Oh, the nagging, the
nagging," she would say, smiling and turning her
face to the heavens as if addressing some angel up
there. "There will be plenty of rest for me when

I'm dead. Nothing but rest for ever. We're going forward. No time to lose."

The nun waddled away, like a big grey bird, and Juana closed her eyes.

When she opened them again, it was dark. How long had she been sleeping? Two candles in tall candlesticks stood on a shelf set high up on the wall and their moving flames threw dark shadows into the corners of her narrow room. Someone was sitting in the chair beside her bed. It wasn't a nun – the headdress was the wrong shape. Perhaps it was someone from their party. Juana strained to sit up.

"Don't be frightened, child."

Juana recognised Eleanor's voice. What was the Old Queen doing here? It must be night-time – she should be asleep.

As though she'd read Juana's thoughts, Eleanor said, "I couldn't sleep, so I thought I'd come and see how you were. Sister Fidelis told me you'd come back to your proper senses."

"Yes," said Juana. "But I keep slipping back into sleep. And dreaming." She didn't dare to say so but part of her wondered if she was in a dream at this very moment: a dream of the queen sitting by her bed.

"You poor child. I hate being sick. Fortunately, I've had good health my whole life. I put it down to my diet when I was small – a great deal of poetry and song. Both, as I'm sure you know, are very good for you. They build up your heart and your mind in the most wondrous way and if your heart and mind are stout, your body will follow their lead."

Juana kept quiet. According to her mama a diet of good milk and fresh eggs was what made you strong, but she wasn't going to contradict the Old Queen. Eleanor, in any case, wasn't listening but rummaging in a small box that she was holding on her lap.

"Are you wondering what I have here?" Eleanor said. "I'll tell you. I'm about to share with you some of my treasure. I keep my most precious possessions in this sandalwood casket."

Juana's eyes widened. *Pearls*, she thought, *or maybe rubies and emeralds and fine gold.* Perhaps there would be rings. Juana loved gemstones and jewellery. Her favourite task, at home, was to help Mama clean and polish the silver goblets and plates used for ceremonial occasions. She said, "Thank you, madam," and struggled to a sitting position, so that she could get a better view of everything.

"This," said Eleanor, "was my first treasure. It was given to me by one of the troubadour poets at my father's court in Aquitaine when I was younger than you. Look!"

Juana looked. The Old Queen was holding out a scrap of parchment, torn along one edge. It was smaller than a page in a missal, smaller than Juana's own hand as she took hold of it.

"Treat this with care," Eleanor said. "It's very old and most precious."

Juana tried to hide her disappointment. Where were the jewels she was expecting? There were some letters scribbled on the parchment. She said, "No one has taught me to read letters, Madam. I don't know what's written here…"

"Oh, how stupid I am! I will read the words to you. No, better yet, I'll sing them. That's how

I first heard them. Benoit sang them… oh, he was a lovely fellow in my father's court and he used to sing to me and the other ladies on summer afternoons in the gardens. I can still bring them to mind – the shady walks, the rose arbours… oh, the fragrance." The Old Queen closed her eyes and began to sing. Her voice was croaky, like something made of metal that hadn't been oiled for a long time.

> *"Come, my rosebud, come my dove,*
> *sit beside me, hear my song.*
> *Listen for these words of love:*
> *it is for thee my heart doth long."*

"Lovely," said Juana. But secretly, she wondered why the Old Queen set any store by such things. Every song in the world that wasn't about war was about love. People were always singing to their ladies. What was precious about that?

Again, it was as though Eleanor had guessed what she was thinking. "It may seem like any old song to you, but to me, it brings back a happy time before my father died. Before I was sent to marry Louis. Oh, the cold Paris court after the warmth and joy of my father's house! You cannot believe how lonely I felt. How homesick. Poor Louis, too! He wasn't much older than me and yet we had to be grown up enough to be married. See this, now."

She reached into the box and brought out a baby's rattle. It looked like a tiny silver ball on a stick, and when she shook it, it made a small, tinkling noise like distant bells.

"This was given to me when I gave birth to my first daughter. Mostly, I try to forget those years, when one daughter after another came from my body and not one of them was any use as an heir to the throne of France. You cannot imagine my fury at the way they treated my daughters – it was as if they were nothing but dolls. The best they might achieve was an alliance with some neighbouring prince. That decided me. I had no intention of being as powerless as they were destined to be."

"What did you do?" Juana was sitting up now, feeling better than she had for a long while.

Listening to Eleanor had made her forget her own troubles.

"I found a way out of my marriage to Louis and wed Henry of England," said the Old Queen. "That gave me more land to rule over. There was a time when I could make Henry do my bidding... and with him I had sons. One of them is Richard, whom you will see before long... oh, he is the handsomest and kindest and bravest boy. But Henry saw Richard as a threat... he locked me up for fifteen years because he thought I was encouraging our son to claim the throne while his father was still alive. Can you imagine such a thing? My own husband, who loved me once upon a time, had me imprisoned in a house in England and I didn't see anyone or travel anywhere for fifteen years. Longer than you've been alive. It was only my box of treasures that kept the dream of somewhere else fresh in my heart. See..."

She reached into it and took out a piece of silk, heavily embroidered with gold threads.

"Is it from a garment, my lady?" Juana asked. "I can see a button hanging there."

"Indeed," Eleanor sighed. "This comes from a robe given to me by my uncle Raymond of Poitiers who ruled in Antioch. In the days when I was still married to Louis, we went on a Crusade. I've never forgotten some of the things we saw. Horrible sights. Battles, dead and dying men, hunger, every kind of sorrow. But also, the blue skies and the beautiful cities of the East, set among the hills and reaching up to heaven with their towers and battlements. The sea, on the way to those shores, heaving in storms and flat as a silver salver in the heat of summer, the birds, the strange smells and foods and other languages. My English prison was not exactly a dungeon, but even a palace is a terrible confinement to someone who longs for a horizon so far away that she can scarcely see it. I hate gates and barriers and locked doors. I want plains and forests and cities and oceans stretching away before me. This robe – it's not a robe now, but it was then – was what I wore in the winter cold in England, over my plainer clothes. I could still smell Raymond's palace at Antioch in the folds of it – spices and lemon and the jasmine blossom's fragrance seemed to be woven into the fabric. Here, hold it to your nose. It seems to me there's still a whiff of all that about it."

Juana held the silk close and sniffed at it. It only smelled like sandalwood – like the inside of the box it had been kept in for so long. She couldn't admit as much to the Old Queen, so she simply smiled and handed it back.

"Poor Raymond!" said Eleanor. "People are so unkind. There were rumours, you know. They said we loved one another, he and I. People are always ready with nasty tales and Louis was upset by them. Ugly rumours, but I shouldn't be telling you of such things. You're much too young. Here is something you'll like, though."

Eleanor took a wooden carving of a rabbit out of the box and laid it on the bed, next to Juana's hand. "That was carved by my son, Richard. I have many sons and daughters and I love them all, of course I do, but Richard... well, he is the special one. It's hard to hide my devotion to him. He is the perfect son. He released me from my prison when Henry died. Richard made this rabbit as a gift for me, when he was only a boy. He whittled at it for hours on end, though I think he was helped by a stonemason engaged in some work at Canterbury Cathedral. Isn't it sweet? You can almost feel how soft the ears are, even though they're made of wood."

Everything the Old Queen had shown her hadn't seemed like treasure, but this rabbit was different. Juana stroked the wooden ears gently with one finger. "I wish I had a carving of Soldado – he's one of the horses in my stable at home… at King Sancho's palace, I mean. I miss him so much."

"I know. I know that feeling… I've been missing one thing or another all my life. If you go from country to country, even if the cause is good and you're creating a kingdom for your children in which they'll be powerful for centuries to come, you never have a proper home. But for the one in that gaol Henry shut me up in, I've never slept in a bed where I haven't thought: *I am only here for a short while*. There's always somewhere to travel to tomorrow. Something else to do. If I don't do things, they don't get done as well by other people. I could have arranged for Berengaria to travel to Richard's court with a party of trusted knights, but alas, I trust no one as much as I trust myself. Even at my age."

Juana spoke before she had time to think. "Do you have other treasure, madam? Jewels, gold, crowns and ornaments?"

"Are you disappointed? I'm sorry… and yes, I do have such things but you can't drag them round with you on your travels and they are only useful when you want to impress the crowds in a procession or sell them to buy weapons for a just war. I scorn such baubles now, though I was dazzled by them at your age. These things…" she patted the box in her lap, "remind me of certain times and certain people. My whole life is here in small memories. My thoughts are my treasure. No one can steal those and no one can truly enjoy them but me. Every single item in this box helps me to remember. At my age, that's what you do most of the time: think of the past." She stood up and smiled at Juana.

"Here," Eleanor said and bent down to lay something on Juana's pillow. "Small enough to put in your own box of treasures when you're older, to remind you of an ancient crone who couldn't sleep one night."

Juana watched, speechless, as the Old Queen left the room. She took the delicate chain, and fastened it round her neck. The tiny silver cross that hung over her nightshirt caught the light from the candles, which had now burned down to short stumps of wax.

My very first treasure, Juana thought. *I must thank the Old Queen tomorrow.*

She lay back on her pillow and fell at once into a deep and healing sleep.

When the royal party set out from the convent, the Old Queen rode astride the leading horse. Juana sat in the last wagon with the other servants, surrounded by chests, and rolled up bundles and baskets which the nuns had packed full of foodstuffs for the journey. She wore the cross Eleanor of Aquitaine had given her around her neck. *Before I set out on this journey*, she thought, *I was afraid of leaving home but now I want to see everything: plains and forests and cities and oceans stretching away before me.*

She looked at the mountains of Northern Italy looming high and pale in the distance and tried to imagine what they would find when they had crossed over them and come down on the other side.

Why I Chose
Eleanor of Aquitaine

My main reason for choosing this queen as my subject is entirely frivolous. In 1968, or maybe 1969, I saw a film called *The Lion in Winter*. It starred the very handsome Peter O'Toole as Henry II and one of my favourite actresses, Katherine Hepburn, as Eleanor. Hepburn won an Oscar for this part. It's years and years ago now, but I remember loving the film, and loving the fierce, intelligent woman that Hepburn was portraying. In researching my story, I found that Eleanor of Aquitaine was truly remarkable in many ways, not least because she lived to be eighty years old at a time when such a thing was most unusual. She reigned over two kingdoms, was wife to two kings and mother to three more. She was a crusader and grew up in a court where the chivalric tradition of courtesy towards women reigned. For all those reasons, I was intrigued by her. In my story, she looks exactly like Katherine Hepburn.

ADÈLE GERAS

Eleanor of Aquitaine Facts

Eleanor (sometimes known as Alienor) of Aquitaine was born in either 1122 or 1124. No one is quite certain of the exact date. She married Louis, King of France, in 1137. Their marriage was annulled because Eleanor had not given birth to a male heir. She had two daughters with him, but no sons. In 1152 she married King Henry II of England. With him she went on a Crusade to the Holy Land. They had five sons and three daughters and three of her sons became kings. Henry imprisoned Eleanor for a long time, because he was angry at his wife's support for their son Richard's claim to his father's crown. Richard I, known as the Lionheart, set his mother free when Henry died and he became king. After Richard's death, the crown of England passed to his brother, King John. Eleanor lived till 1204. She was one of the most powerful women in Europe and her descendants and relations were in control of much of Europe by the beginning of the thirteenth century.

All Shall Be Well

*A Story about Julian of Norwich
(c.1342–c.1416)*

BY KATHERINE LANGRISH

"KNEEL DOWN," says Alys wearily.

So I get down on the floor, trying not to cry. I've done so much kneeling since I came here, I've got overlapping blue and purple bruises on both my knees. They are turning an interesting yellow at the edges; I inspect them when I peel my stockings off and get into bed with Alys at night. I hate sleeping with Alys. She's old and bony, and she complains unless I lie absolutely still, but then she falls asleep ahead of me and snores.

"Apologise for your fault," says Alys, from up above.

I bow my head and clasp my hands across my chest, staring at the hem of her brown worsted gown where it touches the tiles.

"*Mea culpa*," I gulp, "*mea culpa, mea maxima culpa*. I'm sorry I spoke disrespectfully. I'm sorry I was careless. I'm sorry I broke the eggs."

"How did it happen?" Alys sounds calm, but I'm eye level with her hands, and her fingers are twisting and squeezing each other as if she'd like to wring my neck.

"I tripped," I mumble. I was coming down

Conesford Street with the basket of eggs on my arm, and some boys came running past kicking a ball, with dogs chasing the boys and a group of hysterical ducks scattering in their wake. I dodged the boys, the dogs and the ducks, stepped on my own shoelace and went flying. All those lovely golden eggs smashed and dripping! It was a terrible waste. Mother would have slapped my ears. I'd actually prefer that to Alys's tight-lipped disapproval. But Mother isn't here.

Alys starts to scold, low-voiced so as not to disturb Lady Julian, who is saying her prayers in the next room. "You wouldn't have tripped unless you were romping or running. Haven't I told you, over and over again, when I send you out on an errand you are to *walk*? Quietly and modestly?"

"Yes, Alys."

"And to keep your eyes to yourself, not to chatter or gossip or frolic?"

"Yes, Alys."

"You are Lady Julian's maid – what sort of impression do you think people will have of *her* if you rush about, falling over and breaking things?"

I don't answer. It's a stupid question. Lady Julian is far too holy for anyone to think badly of her just because of me.

"You don't seem sorry at all," Alys sighs. "You'd better stay there on your knees while you say three Paternosters, and *think*. Think how to be a better girl. Think about your sins."

There are Seven Deadly Sins painted on the chancel wall of the church, and I seem to have most of them. Sloth, for one – Alys says I should do my work joyfully and eagerly, but I don't. I do my work all right, but I begrudge it. Wrath – I'm angry at least once a day, and I *hate* Richard, my stepfather. Then there's Envy... I'm jealous of my sister Annot. That makes three of the seven already. I need to stop, this is scary. At least I can truthfully say Lust doesn't bother me. But Gluttony – I can't help thinking about food. We eat only vegetable stew here, and I'm longing for a bite of meat. I dream of spiced sausages bursting out of their skins, and wake up hungry. Alys says, "You'll get used to it, it's just Greed."

Finally, Pride. Pride is the worst of all, the sin of Lucifer. It hardens your heart. It stops you feeling sorry for the bad things you've done.

Like now.

"Finished?" asks Alys briskly. "Then get up and be useful."

She sets me to preparing vegetables, which means I can wipe my eyes and pretend it's only the onions making me cry.

There's a soft scratching at the inner door. Alys opens it and I hear Lady Julian's low voice, asking something. Alys murmurs in reply, glancing at me. What are they saying? Is the lady asking about me? Alys gives me a look that says, *None of your business, get on with your work*, and disappears inside Lady Julian's cell, shutting the door behind her.

Everyone in Norwich knows about Lady Julian, though hardly anyone ever sees her. She's our anchoress, holier than any nun. When she was just a young woman she fell sick, so sick she nearly died. As she lay there suffering, her eyes dimming, the sweat of death cold on her face, who should appear to her in a vision but our blessed Lord Jesus himself?

And she got better.

If a miracle like that happened to me, I'd dance and sing and cry for joy. I'd go to church, of course, and thank our blessed Lord, and I'd – I don't know – I'd give the best thing I could to the church, a silver penny or a big fat candle. But I wouldn't, I *couldn't* do what she did next. She went to the bishop and asked to be locked up in the little cell at the back of St Julian's Church so that she could spend the rest of her life there, praying. And he agreed. So one day more than twenty years ago, she came here, and the bishop said the funeral service over her and sprinkled her with earth, as if she was already dead. Then she walked calmly into that inner room, and they shut the door on her, and she's not come out again. Never, not once. And she never will. Not till the day she dies and they carry her out to the burying ground.

How can she bear it?

I'm looking at her door now. It's as thick and heavy as the one in the church porch. I've been through it once. I had to. She wanted to see me last month when I first came. I trembled from head to foot, I felt as if I were visiting a holy tomb. Maybe angels visit her when the door is shut. But she's only a bent old woman in a black gown and a white veil, like a nun. She moves slowly, as if her joints are stiff. Her eyes are pale blue and the skin of her hands and face is very pale too, like soft, crumpled leather. She welcomed me quietly. I think she does everything quietly. I wonder if she ever danced or jumped or sang in all her life? Proper songs, I mean, not psalms. Songs you sing because you're happy and for no other reason, as we did at home.

Oh, it was lovely on winter evenings when mother would sit knitting at one side of the fire, rocking baby Margery (who died) or baby Hugh (he died too), and my father and Annot and I would sit at the other, and we'd sing carols and rounds: 'Wed Me, Robin, and Bring Me Home' and 'I Have Twelve Oxen' and 'Blow Northern Wind, Send Me My Sweeting'. And darling Tib, my little white cat, would curl, purring, on my lap. I miss Tib. She was due to have kittens when

I left home. I wish there were a little cat here to cuddle. I've dropped hints. But Alys doesn't listen.

What does Lady Julian do all day, shut up in her cell? Alys says she is writing a book about all the visions she had. I never heard of a woman writing a book! And of course she prays. She prays all the time, special prayers like the monks, not just the Paternoster and the Ave Maria like ordinary folk.

Her prayers work, too. One night just after I came, I woke up to see a skinny little imp skipping around the room, twirling his tail and dancing and making rude gestures. He was so comical I laughed out loud and he turned in a flash. "Oho!" he said. "*You* don't belong here!" And he jumped right at my face, grinning. I shrieked and fought with the bedclothes, and then Alys was saying, "Good heavens, child, don't thrash so!" and the imp was gone. Alys went back to sleep, but I lay stiff with fright, thinking he might return, till I saw candlelight from the cracks of Lady Julian's door and realised she was awake, praying. That must be why the imp had fled. But I'm still worried.

I know the imp spoke the truth when he said, "*You don't belong here!*" So where *do* I belong? Not at home any more.

Last spring it rained for all of Lent – cold sleeting rain, driving in from the German Sea on a harsh east wind. Father had to be out in it, dawn till dusk, muck-spreading, ditching, raking, ploughing, then coming home chilled and soaked. By Candlemas he was coughing so hard it hurt to hear, and by St Gregory's Day he was dead. We'd prayed so hard, I'd thought God might give *us* a miracle, but no. Mother says she's wept enough tears to know that miracles don't come two a penny.

Right, I've finished the onions. Peeled and chopped the turnips. Cleaned the leeks. Put them all in water. Set the dried peas to soak. And I'm hungry, hungry, hungry. It's only mid-morning; we got up at dawn, as always, and we won't eat till noon. There's a small bowl of apples on the deep windowsill, a present for Lady Julian from one of the townsmen. My mouth waters just looking at them, but it would be stealing to take one, and even if I'm a sinner, I'm not a thief. Alys won't allow 'munching' between meals. But I nibble one hard little pea that's dropped on the table. It's dry and bitty, but I chew it up anyway. That can't be stealing, can it? Maybe it is. Maybe I *will* go to hell. And then our priest can hold me up as a terrible example. The Girl Who Went to Hell Because She Stole a Dried Pea.

Alys is still in there with Lady Julian. I'm feeling more and more nervous. What can they be talking about? It must be about me. Whatever will I do if the lady sends me away? I can't go home. I don't *have* a home. Not now.

Mother was never as easy-going as Father, and after he died she became very short-tempered and stern. I think she was worried about money. Under the terms of our lease, she had to find a man to work the land for her. She couldn't do it on her own. I thought she would hire a ploughman, but of course she would have to pay him, and then our neighbour Richard de Wotton offered to marry her, and to my horror she said yes. How? Why? How *could* she?

He is a lean, hollow man with shaggy eyebrows and spindly legs, long knobbly fingers and a perpetual sniff. He said, "Well, Joan, I know you are an honest, thrifty woman." *Sniff.* "And it makes good sense for us to marry – my land at Butterhills runs next to yours." *Sniff.* "As for the children, Annot will stay at home, but the eldest is big enough to earn her own keep. What is she, twelve? My cousin Alys, the anchoress's woman, needs a girl to run errands and do the rough work. It would be a good place for Sarah. Shall I speak to Alys?"

I will never forgive him. I looked at Mother, certain she would refuse. I thought she would jump up and exclaim, "Lose my Sarah? Never!" and order him out of the house. Not a bit! She just nodded and said, "That will be very kind of you, Richard."

So I was sent away. I always knew Annot was her favourite. They are all together, *him* and Mother and Annot and my darling little Tib – they have each other and I have nobody. I must stay here till I'm withered and old like Alys and the lady, never singing anything but psalms, never running or skipping or dancing, never going anywhere except on an errand 'and coming straight back', never going a-Maying, never...

I want to feel Mother's arms around me and put my head on her shoulder. I want to see Annot's teasing smile. I want to stroke Tib and feel her soft, soft fur...

I will not cry.

The latch of the lady's door lifts with a loud click. My heart skips a beat. Alys comes out, looking rather quiet and strange. "The lady wants to see you." Her eyes are red-rimmed. I stare at her, petrified, and she says sharply, "Did you not hear me?" and then, more gently, "Go along, Sarah, and don't be afraid."

So I rub my hands quickly on my gown and pull my cap straight, and tap. "Come in," says the lady's low voice, and I slide in around the door, my heart beating hard.

It's a dark little stone room, so small I could cross it in three hops. The only daylight comes through a tiny round window high up on the east wall. Under it there's a small altar with a crucifix. A narrow north window looks slantwise into the church, so she can peek in and see the Blessed Sacrament. And one more window faces south into the churchyard, but it's covered with shutters and a black cloth. There's a fireplace with a chimney, a bed with a chamber pot under it, and in the middle of the floor there's a tall sloping desk. That's all.

I bob my head to Lady Julian, but I'm gulping. It's hard to breathe. These four walls are all she ever sees, day in, day out. In more than twenty years she hasn't seen the sun rising out of the mist on the water meadows, or white summer dust rolling in clouds behind the wheels of an ox cart, or stars glittering in the night sky, or the wind ruffling the surface of the river, or the bluebells coming up in Thorpe Wood...

"Sarah," she says gently. "Alys thinks you are unhappy. Are you still grieving for your father?"

"Yes, but..." A huge lump rises in my throat. I feel worse than ever. I *am* grieving for him, of course, but mostly I'm unhappy because of other things. I don't understand myself. I'm like a fish out of water, flapping and gasping.

"I'm wicked," I blurt. "I don't know why I'm so wicked, but I am. I'm lazy and bad, and even when Alys makes me *say* I'm sorry, I'm not, I just pretend. I'm so wicked I don't even *want* to be sorry! So I know I'm going to hell."

Her eyes open wide. "Goodness, child, no wonder you're unhappy! You're not wicked at all. You're hurt and you're angry. I can see it glowing in you, like a little fiery coal that you're carrying about. You nurse it and blow on it to keep it bright. No wonder you're in pain! Let go of it, Sarah. It is scorching a hole in your heart."

I start to cry. "I don't know how! I'm not like you! *You* had a vision of our Lord. *I* saw a little black imp who told me I don't belong here! And I don't. I don't belong anywhere. Mother doesn't love me any more. She likes Annot better than me. Why did she have to marry Richard de Wotton? Why did she keep Annot and send me away? Why do bad things happen? Why did our Lord send a miracle for you and not for Father, even though we prayed and prayed for him? I want things to be as they were. I can't bear to stay here for ever and never go home!"

"Sarah, Sarah!" Her arms are around me. "Where shall I start? Is that what you thought? That you must stay here for ever?"

"Alys has," I sob.

"Alys stays because she loves me and because she wants to, not because she has to!" She gives me a little shake. "As for the imp? *Retro, Sathanas* – be gone, Satan! I too have seen the devil. He is a liar! He is nothing! We will not listen to him! For the rest, Richard de Wotton is not a bad man. He and your mother haven't sent you away for ever. In a year or two, they will send Annot here as well, and if you want to, you will go home. In the meantime, they know you are safe here. You will learn to read and write, which will be a great advantage to you. They mean well, Sarah!"

"Why didn't they tell me this?" I wail.

"Why didn't you ask? Perhaps they thought you knew." She shakes me again. Her face is very serious. "Listen. You must trust the people you love!

When I was still young – though you would think me old – I was given the best gift you could ever imagine. I saw and spoke with our blessed Lord! But I was just like you. I couldn't understand why there is so much pain and suffering in the world. So I asked him. Me! I dared to ask our Lord! And he answered me! Think of it!"

"What… did he say?" I hiccup.

"Come here." She leads me to her desk. There's a book propped on it, open. "Can you read at all?"

"I know the ABC." I peer at it in awe. "Did *you* write all of this?"

She nods. "Yes, and I have not yet finished. It is called *The Showings of God's Love*. See if you can spell this line."

I take a deep breath and cross myself. The letters dance before my eyes, but I recognise a great *A*, and next to it a little looping *l*. Then a snaky *s*, and *h* like a house with a chimney, and then *a* and *l* again. Slowly I spell out the whole line. "*All… shall… b-be … well.*"

I look at her. "'All shall be well?' Is that what our Lord told you?"

Her crumpled old cheek is close to mine. She looks into my eyes and nods.

"How *can* it be well?" I burst out. "When terrible things happen, and people die, and the priest says some people go to hell for ever—"

Lady Julian holds up a finger. "I do not know," she says firmly. "So I keep on asking and wondering, and that is what my book is all about. But even if I don't understand His answer, I trust it, Sarah, because our Blessed Lord loves us. And what seems impossible to us may be very easy for Him. He has promised me – *all shall be well, and all shall be well, and all manner of things shall be well.*"

She stops. It's very quiet in here. Cool and peaceful. The candle flame flickers. It makes a soft purring, fluttering sound, like a butterfly at a window. I gather up my courage.

"Then… may I ask you something else?"

"Of course, my child."

"Can we… Would you…" I stop, twisting my fingers in my gown. "At home, we have a little white cat. She's a very good mouser! And she was expecting kittens when I left. And—"

Lady Julian is laughing – actually laughing! "Now strangely enough," she says, "the one animal I am allowed to keep is a cat, but my last died a year ago. I have decided it is time we acquired another. I shall send a message to your mother and ask that the next time Richard de Wotton rides into Norwich, she shall come with him and bring us one of those white kittens. Now, off you go. Wash your face and hands. Then run outside and say your prayers in God's good sunshine."

So I do. The sun is warm on my back. The bees are booming in the elm tree at the corner of the churchyard. The swallows are building nests under the church eaves and flashing low over the grass.

And I run, and I jump, and I sing.

Why I Chose Julian of Norwich

I wanted to write about Lady Julian of Norwich because she's one of the most fascinating and mysterious of medieval women! She comes across in her writing as an intelligent, questioning person who actually challenges God about the existence of suffering and pain (she lived through the Black Death, so I imagine she would have known plenty about both).

It would seem a very odd decision today, to spend your whole life in one small room. It was unusual in medieval times, too. Only strong personalities could cope with it. I wanted to write a story about Lady Julian in which I could imagine her – a strong, compassionate woman – living a strange, hard life, but one she chose for herself and never regretted.

KATHERINE LANGRISH

Julian of Norwich Facts

Julian of Norwich was probably born in 1342. There is so much we don't really know about her – we don't know exactly when she was born or when she died, if she was ever married or had children, or who her parents were. We can't even be sure of her real name. Thanks to her writing however, we *do* know that in May 1373, when she was 'thirty and a half years old', she fell so ill she was expected to die. While ill, she experienced a series of sixteen visions of Christ's suffering on the cross, after which she was healed. She wrote two accounts of these visions, called *The Showings of God's Love*, the first of which was the very first book known to have been written by a woman in English.

At some point, Julian became a holy anchoress – a person who retires from the world like a hermit, to live and pray alone in one tiny cell or small room. Lady Julian's cell was attached to the church of St Julian and St Edward's, in Norwich, and this may be why we know her as 'Julian'. Anchoresses were expected to pray much of the time, like nuns, but they also provided spiritual and mental comfort and advice – rather like the medieval version of a psychiatrist. Julian's mixture of faith, mysticism and common sense made her famous in her own city of Norwich and people came to visit her from other towns too.

Lady Julian of Norwich died in around 1416. Her writing is still widely read today and has had much influence on Christian thought.

Learn to Die

*A story about Lady Jane Grey
(1537–54)*

BY MARY HOFFMAN

THE DARK-HAIRED MAN GRIPPED the rail of the ship, but not in fear of the waves. He could not believe that he was at last seeing the coast of England disappearing in the distance. It was the second time he had fled from a country to escape execution for his religion, but this time, he had a wife and small child to think about.

They were huddled below deck, feeling sick, and as soon as the last sight of England had faded, the man went down to join them, taking his son in his arms and kissing his head. Let the boy sleep till they reached the coast of France – he would watch over him. Some people you could save, even if others had gone beyond your reach.

— ❋ —

They were just three little girls when I met them in 1550: the brains, the beauty and the determined one. Mind you, they were all strong-willed, though Katherine, the middle daughter, was a lot more easy-going than her sisters. I was to teach the two older girls Italian; they were already fluent in

French and Latin, with Jane knowing Greek too.

Lady Jane Grey was thirteen years old and small for her age but her mind was impressive. She already preferred books and learning to hunting and dancing.

At first, she was stiff and formal in all our lessons and I preferred her pretty, laughing little sister Katherine. But gradually, Jane thawed towards me, especially when she discovered just how much I shared her views about the new religion.

And once she started to talk to me properly, I found out that she had already lived through more troubled times than most women twice her age. I hadn't paid all that much attention to events in England in the last few years. I'd been in prison in Rome for two of them.

Then Jane told me about Catherine Parr.

"She was a second mother to me," she said. "And much less strict than my real one."

It was true that Jane's mother was a rather stern figure. She was always pleasant to me though. And her husband, the Marquis, was positively good company.

"I had so many beautiful new dresses when I lived with Catherine at Seymour Place," Jane told me. "And a woman just to dress my hair."

I couldn't imagine serious little Jane being entranced by such things. The first time I met her, she surprised me by telling me she could say 'learn to die' in half a dozen languages. Her first tutor had thought that all Christian children should be given such stern sentences to translate. But, once she started talking about Catherine, she seemed much less reserved.

"She was the kindest, warmest person I have ever met," she said sadly. "And so in love with… with *him*."

Jane's brown eyes glittered when she mentioned this man, but not from love or grief, as I learned later.

"Catherine had been queen – you know that, don't you?" she said.

"Just assume I know nothing about the court, my lady," I said.

"She was Henry's last queen," said Jane. "And married her next husband in secret, very soon after the king died."

"That was the *him* she was so in love with?"

"Thomas Seymour, the Baron of Sudeley," said Jane, looking as if the very name tasted bad in her mouth.

"Why are you so bitter about him? Did he harm you?"

"Not me. But he was my guardian and he should have protected my reputation. Did you know he paid my father two thousand pounds to have me living with them?"

I was shocked at such a sum – what he had been buying for that two thousand pounds? I was never able to understand English politics.

"He was a flirt," said Jane. "And a rogue. But very handsome. Catherine adored him and soon she was carrying his child."

It was enough to make a religious man like me blush to hear such a young girl talk of such things, but I wanted to know what the flirty rogue had done to win her disapproval. Her mouth had shrivelled like a prune when she'd said his name.

"He was the old king's brother-in-law."

"Ah. You know I get confused by all those wives."

"He was the new king's uncle, brother to his mother, Jane Seymour."

"You say he *was*. He is dead?"

"They say the king will soon have no uncles," said Jane. "He beheaded Thomas Seymour two years ago but I would put no wager on Edward Seymour – Thomas's brother – keeping his head on his shoulders for long. He has already been imprisoned in the Tower once."

I shuddered. What a country had I found myself in! Had I fled the death sentence in Rome only to find myself in a nest of murderers and fanatics? And little Jane was so calm about it – maybe this was how noble people treated life and death?

"I'm sure it was his treachery and faithlessness that killed poor Catherine Parr," Jane told me.

"You are talking about Thomas Seymour?"

"He behaved disgracefully with my cousin Elizabeth, who was another of his wards. Going into her bedchamber and tickling her and romping under the bedclothes when he was only half-dressed and bare-legged. And she, King Edward's sister! But maybe that's why the baron was interested in her?"

Was this the way young ladies of the English aristocracy talked? Even though Jane clearly disapproved and was too pure and prim to behave that way herself.

"And then when Catherine was heavy with Seymour's child, she found him trying to kiss and cuddle Elizabeth, so my cousin was sent away."

She looked really sad now.

"I didn't miss Elizabeth – she was always very cold to me – but I'd rather Thomas had been sent away instead. I had to go to Gloucestershire with poor Catherine, who was weeping her eyes out, and wait with her until her child was born."

"What happened to Seymour?"

"Oh, he came for the birth. It was a little girl. But Catherine was dead within the week. And they had the most tremendous rows in those last days – shouting and crying – I'm sure that's what killed her."

"Where is the child now?"

"Dead, like both her parents."

I soon learned that, though he had died nearly three years ago, Thomas Seymour still played an active part in the household of the Marquis of Dorset, Henry Grey. Seymour's great scheme had been to marry his young ward Jane to the new king. They had played together as children and now, old enough to be betrothed, they shared the same serious approach to ideas and religion. It seemed that Thomas Seymour's plan might work after all.

The marquis would have liked that. He was about my age, with as dark a beard as mine but a florid English colour to his face. I don't know if he was more ambitious than he was vain; the gossips said he liked to be referred to as 'prince' in private. And within a year of my coming to teach the Grey girls Italian, their father was already a much more important person than when he first employed me.

It came about because of a tragedy in the

family. Two little boys died on the same day in July – of the sweating sickness – and at a blow the male heirs to the title Duke of Suffolk were wiped out. They were Jane's late grandfather's children by his last wife, and great favourites of my lady. But by the autumn, the tragedy had turned to advantage for Henry Grey, when the young king gave him the title of Duke of Suffolk. In fact, now that I look back towards England and the past, I see that day as the beginning of all Lady Jane's troubles.

That was the day I saw King Edward for the first time. He was a slight figure, with hair as burnished gold as an angel's, not exactly kingly, but with a good presence for one so young. He would have made a good match for Lady Jane.

But it was not to be.

Henry Grey and his friend John Dudley, recently invested with the title Duke of Northumberland and a frequent visitor to the Grey household, had other ideas.

It was still winter when I found my lady in tears. I thought at first she wept for Edward Seymour, Thomas's brother, who had just been executed – as Jane had predicted – at the Tower of London.

"No, I do not waste a tear on another Seymour," she said, fiercely brushing her eyes with her handkerchief. "But my sister's maid has told her and she has told me that it is all over the servants' quarters that... I am to be married."

Servants hear a lot when lords regard them as no more important than a bucket.

"Should I congratulate you, my lady?"

"I don't want to marry Guildford Dudley!"

The Duke of Northumberland's son. It had surprised me that this was what the two dukes had been plotting – not marriage to the king.

"Is he not a handsome choice?" I asked.

I had seen young Dudley and he was a good-looking youth of sixteen, tall and fair-haired.

Lady Jane fixed me with one of her sternest stares.

"He is a fourth son! And I've heard I am his second choice. The rumours are that he wanted to marry my cousin Margaret but she wouldn't have him. Or at least her father wouldn't have the

Duke of Northumberland. After all, marriages aren't made between bride and groom in families like ours."

I had never heard her so bitter. Perhaps she was disappointed at the thought of not being Queen of England after all? She was certainly much changed from the little maid who had delighted in the gorgeous gowns that Catherine Parr had given her, preferring instead to dress very simply and usually in black. Her sister Katherine had told me that the Lady Mary, the king's sister, had sent Jane a most beautiful dress of gold and silver cloth at Christmas, yet Jane had just said, "What am I to do with this?" and put on one of her old plain robes.

"She could have given it to me at least," Katherine, who at eleven, was far less pious than her older sister, had wailed.

But Jane had tremendous self-control; she soon recovered her composure and concentrated on the day's lesson.

It wasn't till the next year that the rumours of her betrothal surfaced again. By this time it was clear that the young king would not live to be married to Jane or anyone else; he was still only fifteen but had never recovered from the terrible illness of the lungs he fell sick with at the beginning of the year. Was that why she accepted Dudley? I don't think she was any happier about the idea than she had been the year before, but the pressure from her father and Northumberland was too great to resist.

"My little sister Mary and I are to be married too," said young Katherine, with much more enthusiasm than her elder sister had ever shown.

There was a betrothal in April and by the end of May, Jane was married to Dudley and Katherine to the son of the Earl of Pembroke. I was pleased to see two of my young pupils wed. Little Mary was too young at eight to be more than betrothed but I was glad of that, as the husband chosen for her was a grizzled old soldier with a terrible wound on his face.

Once she was a married woman I ceased to teach Jane; she was now living with her husband's family at Durham House. But one day she sent for me in my capacity as chaplain. I was no longer a pastor at my church because my child was conceived out of wedlock, but Jane and I shared beliefs and she knew she could trust me.

Jane had momentous news.

"It seems Northumberland has found another way to have Edward make me queen," she said, after first ensuring we were alone and not overheard. "The king leaves his crown to me and my male heirs."

"Male heirs?" I said, shocked by the extent of Northumberland's influence over the dying king. "There is little time for you to have one of those. I think you will be queen very soon, my lady," I said and went to kneel to her.

"Don't!" she said sharply and then put her face in her hands. "I don't want it and I don't seek it. But I know you will understand that I think perhaps God is calling me to that duty. To preserve the new religion. Think what would happen if the king's half-sister Mary became queen instead. She would outlaw all the changes the king has made."

Neither of us mentioned Edward's other half-sister, Elizabeth, but she was on our minds. Whoever knew what that haughty princess really thought? But, at least she was closer in her religious views to the dying king than his other sister would ever be.

"Both sisters are confirmed illegitimate," said Jane. "And Edward won't name them as heirs. He is happy that I am married to an Englishman already and can't be ruled by a foreign husband as they might be."

Even then I could see what a dangerous road lay ahead for this young girl. She was just sixteen and the powerful men around her – her father and father-in-law first among them wanted to press this heavy weight on her, not just of a royal crown but of all the warring factions in England.

"We are to move from here," said Jane, setting her shoulders determinedly. "We are to live in Catherine Parr's house in Chelsea."

"You will be happy there?"

"Perhaps."

Within days, King Edward was dead. He was

not quite sixteen. When the Privy Council went to tell Jane she was queen, she wept at the weight of her responsibilities.

I was honoured to accompany Jane and Dudley on the barge to the Tower. She was wearing a green velvet gown, all printed in gold, and wore a white headdress covered in jewels. Dudley stood beside her, dressed in silver and white. They made a handsome couple, but so young! As the barge reached the Tower and the great guns sounded, I felt afraid to hear this small figure of a girl-woman proclaimed queen. No one cheered and my heart felt icy within me.

I had to return home to my wife, who was close to her time. In the days that followed, news of the outside world reached me sporadically, as I became a father for the first time. My son Giovanni – John in the English tongue – was a healthy, bawling child, eager for milk.

Later I heard that in this short time as monarch, Jane showed her strong will when the

Privy Councillors suggested making a crown for her husband.

'Why?' she had asked. "He won't be king. I'll make him a duke, if you like, but nothing higher. If I am queen then I intend to rule as one, not have a husband make my decisions for me."

But soon news came that made such choices beside the point. The Lady Mary had declared herself queen and was gathering supporters all over the country. Jane was a usurper, according to Mary, and the 'rightful monarch' was now heading to London with a great train of armed followers.

Just nine days after Jane had been proclaimed queen, Mary was accepted by all, including the treacherous Dukes of Northumberland and Suffolk, Jane's own family. The Tower had changed from a royal palace to a prison for Jane and her husband.

I begged to be allowed to visit her, something that later put me in my present danger. I found her calm.

"If I am to die, so be it," she said. "I would rather lose my life than return to the old religion with its crucifixes and cannibalism!"

She was truly a woman young in years and old in wisdom.

My lady's mother, the duchess, pleaded with the new queen for the life of her daughter and husband. They were old friends, in spite of their religious differences. And it might have worked, if the duke hadn't plotted again to put Jane back on the throne.

Suffolk headed a rebellion against Mary's planned marriage to the king of Spain. Some people believe I was involved in it but I wasn't. The only evidence against me was my love for Queen Jane, as I will still call her, and for the beliefs we shared.

There was only one possible outcome, once the rebel forces had been defeated. Jane would not change her religion, even though Queen Mary sent her own chaplain to persuade her.

I felt so proud of my lady's bravery when I heard this. It would have saved her life to change but she was too steadfast for that.

Jane and her husband were beheaded on the same day, 12th February. Just a few weeks ago. And her father soon followed. Jane had given me her Greek New Testament to take to her sister Katherine, with the message: "Labour always and learn to die." It was a lesson she had been learning herself for years, as I now see.

England is too dangerous for me now. So I am seeking safety for my family abroad. Who knows what the future may bring? Will someone save that poor country from the Popish religion that Jane chose to die rather than accept? Whatever happens, there will be much blood spilled and if I stay it might be my beautiful son that suffers for my beliefs one day.

— ❈ —

The dark man's son stirred in his arms while the mother still slept, worn out by their sea-voyage.

The man looked out of the porthole that now showed the shore of France coming closer, and tears coursed down his face. Just remembering his pupil Lady Jane Grey filled him with pride at her bravery and deep sadness at her fate. He would never forget her until his dying day.

Why I Chose Lady Jane Grey

The Tudors never seem to be out of fashion! But rather than write about Henry VIII or Queen Elizabeth I, I felt drawn to this teenage girl who was so serious about her religion. Some people have described her as a pawn pushed about on the political chessboard by her powerful and ambitious supporters. I don't buy that. Or the sentimental image of her as pathetic victim in the famous painting by Delaroche.

Jane Grey strikes me as a very determined young woman, willing to die rather than convert to Queen Mary's Catholicism. It is a tragedy that she had to live up to that conviction, and so young, but I think she knew what she was doing and what the likely outcome would be.

MARY HOFFMAN

Lady Jane Grey Facts

Lady Jane Grey was born in 1537, though there is some disagreement about the month. The latest scholarship seems to favour May. She was the eldest daughter of Frances Brandon, the niece of Henry VIII, and Henry Grey, the Marquis of Dorset, who was later made Duke of Suffolk. The Grey sisters received a very good education and Jane was taught Italian by Michelangelo Florio, the narrator of this story. His son John later came back to England and became a friend of the Earl of Southampton; John probably knew William Shakespeare. Under the terms of Edward VI's will, Jane was to inherit the throne and continue his religious reforms. When Edward died in 1553, his Privy Council, which included Jane's father and father-in-law, told her she was queen and she went to the Tower of London to prepare for her coronation.

Jane's period as queen was short-lived and she is often known as 'the nine days queen'. Edward's elder half-sister Mary claimed the throne and had much more popular support. After more plots and rebellions, Jane and her young husband were executed in 1554. Jane was only sixteen when she died.

The Phoenix Bride

A story about Elizabeth Stuart
(1596–1662)

BY DIANNE HOFMEYR

'Up then fair phoenix bride, frustrate the sun.'
John Donne

5TH NOVEMBER, 1605

THE CARRIAGE WHEELS SHUDDER through deep
ruts. We travel with speed. Crouched on the floor
in the darkness, we are jostled hard. I stretch up
to peep around the heavy cloth drawn across the
window. A sliver of moon tears at ragged clouds.
If it rains now and we lodge in the mud, we are
doomed. Soon it will be daylight.

Ann's voice is close to my ear. "Don't worry, my
lady. We'll escape."

I grip Ann's hand. "Tell me again what you
overheard."

"Your father, the king, and your brother, Henry
– who was to accompany him to Parliament – are
safe. The villain was discovered before harm was
done. He was disguised as a coalman and standing
amidst an abundance of gunpowder, in the bowels
of Westminster, ready with a lantern and a slow
match to blow the place to smithereens on the day

of the Opening of Parliament."

"If he's already caught, why are we fleeing?"

"There's more to the plot."

"*More?*"

"I heard the names Robert Catesby and the Wright brothers. They planned to lure your guardian from Coombe Abbey on the pretence of a stag hunt, so they could——"

But the horses swerve. There are muffled shouts. The sound of heavy gates swinging open. Hooves clip cobblestone.

Ann twitches the curtain. "We are here!"

"Where?"

"Within the walls of Coventry."

I grab her by the shoulder. "Go on. So they could – *what?*"

But we are interrupted again as the horses pull up abruptly. The doors of the carriage are flung open. We are lifted out by pikemen and set down next to the stamping, snorting horses whose eyes are wild and whose nostrils flare with foam. There is no time to take in my surroundings. We are hurried through the dark with the sharp clip of metal-capped boots against cobble and the clank of armour. Flares of light catch on the sharp tips of the men's pikes but their faces are in shadow. No word is spoken.

I find myself in a dark hall hung with tapestries. I hear the thud of a heavy door and a bolt being thrown into place behind us. The metal-capped boots march off. At the far end the only light comes from a huge fire burning in a stone hearth. A panel of carved Tudor roses is thrown into heavy relief with the words PALACE YARD carved above them. Clusters of pale-faced maids stand about the hall. Eyes darting about. Hands fidgeting.

Something is amiss. I spin around to confront Ann. "What haven't you told me?"

She shakes her head. "You're not supposed to know."

"Know what?"

She whispers close to my ear. "They plan to steal you."

"*Steal* me? Who?"

"The men who planned the stag hunt to lure

your guardian away – Catesby, the Wright brothers and some other Warwickshire men. They're Catholics. They want you for a *Catholic* queen."

"*Me?* Elizabeth Stuart? A Catholic queen? But I'm a Protestant. And besides I'm much too young to be queen."

"They plan to marry you to a Catholic prince. So your guardian rides out to capture them. And here behind the walls of Coventry, you are safe."

Despite the warmth of the fire, I shiver.

Ann pulls me close. "Don't worry. The plan is foiled. The 5th day of November in the year of our Lord, 1605, will be remembered for ever. The king and your brother are safe. And so are you."

"What a queen I would be by such means! I'd rather have died alongside them in the Houses of Parliament."

AUTUMN, 1609

I have come to make my farewells. I have loved each bird and given each a pet name.

I halt my horse in front of my favourite,

Flamboyant – named for his bright green and red plumage. He was brought back alive from a hot land but died in the cold mists of England. Even the work of the most artful taxidermist could not revive his splendour. Now he is bedraggled and pinned to a tree. The rain and wind have taken the sheen from his feathers and the glint from his eyes.

I sweep the French hood back from my face. "Farewell, Flamboyant."

My breath comes out in puffs against the cold air. This garden was once my classroom. My guardian fixed maps and drawings next to each bird that died, to tell me of the exotic places they once came from.

Swans glide across the mirrored lake. There's no time to take the rowboat to the island but I see the dome of the aviary glistening with its mosaic of glass pieces. I think of my other birds still alive, perched on branches behind the gold mesh. The song of a Golden Oriole pierces the silence. She is calling for her mate.

"Lady Elizabeth," Ann tugs at my cloak.

"Pull up your hood before you are recognised. Your chamber women will find your bed empty and your grooms will discover three horses gone – then what? You've said your farewells. We must hurry. We've a long journey ahead today."

My breath seems sucked from my body. The abbey has been my childhood home. I think of all I'm leaving behind – my aviary, the midwinter breakfasts by candlelight, the games of shuttlecock, the feasts of marchpane smuggled to us by the pastry cook, even the tapestries of beasts around my bed and my farthingale armchair with its Turkey work done by my ladies.

"I'll miss Coombe."

"There's no time for sadness. You're going to court to find a suitor. Your beloved brother, Henry, will be there." Ann blushes as she says his name. She is tongue-tied in the presence of my brother. "Henry will be at Richmond. You at Kew. Your parents at Whitehall. With tournaments and banquets and masques devised by your mother, you'll see him often."

"So will you!"

She blushes all the more.

I give her a teasing smile. "Don't worry. I'll write to him. I'll banish those lists of ugly princesses they plan for him to marry – especially the de' Medici with their daughter Christina. My brother will *never* marry a Catholic."

Throughout my stay at Coombe, I have written to my brother. Letters tied with coloured strands of silk floss – royal blue, grass green and amethyst – twisted with silver thread and sealed with my Scots lion rampart. Letters in different inks – even gold – in different styles of writing as was my mood, and often in French or Italian to impress him. He sometimes answered. Sometimes didn't.

"Here! Thomas! Make a stirrup of your hands so we may get down."

I step into my groom's cupped hands. He keeps his eyes lowered perhaps because of my chemise but out of the corner of my eye I notice he takes Ann by the waist as he lifts her down.

"Give me your dagger, Thomas."

"My dagger, your ladyship?"

"You heard. Is it sharp?"

"Honed to perfection to protect your ladyship."

"I'm glad you are both coming to court with me." I stab the tip into the flesh of my middle finger. A garnet of blood forms. "Hold out your finger, Ann." I grip it and stab. "Now press against mine. Swear by our joined blood you will be my friend for ever."

Thomas is smiling.

"I should make *you* swear, Thomas, not to tell my minders of this morning's escapade."

"My lips are sealed, your ladyship, without the need for blood."

"Good! Then help me on to my horse again. We will race each other back to the abbey. I'll wager that neither of you win. A string of pearls if you do."

SEPTEMBER, *1610*

Once we are settled at Kew, Ann and I see Henry often. We attend banquets, tournaments and masques where he appears as a most handsome

Oberon, in a costume designed by Mr Inigo Jones. And Henry has a ship built – the *Prince Royal.* It's England's largest man-of-war. The letters *HP* – Henry, Prince of Wales – are embossed on the bow, alongside the white plumes of his insignia. The figurehead of St George stretches out from the bowsprit.

We assemble at the Woolwich dockyard for its launch. My father is moody – his stomach troubled by dining on too many grapes. My mother is wearing one of her most elaborate wigs, bedecked with rubies and pearls. Difficult to cope with in such a wind. I want to laugh but I dare not. She has taken her dressing very seriously. So has Ann, for different reasons.

The high wind is keeping out the tide. The ship is stuck and will remain so until the wind calms. My heart aches for Henry. He has set great store by this day. Our party and all the attendants return to Greenwich Palace, but Henry stays behind with the Lord Admiral. I look back and see him standing there with the gilt cup still full of the wine that was to be used to name his ship.

I would calm the winds for him, if I could. I would stamp the ocean flat and call in the tide.

In the same month of September I receive my first proposal. It comes from the king of Sweden. He is eager for a bride for his son, Gustavus Adolphus.

And so it begins. I move from Kew to Hampton Court to receive the ambassadors of my suitors. Portraits arrive in advance. Ann and I pore over the miniatures as we hide between the clipped hedges of the maze.

I shrug. "I'm fifteen. Perhaps too old? Perhaps like my godmother Elizabeth, the past queen, I'll never marry."

Ann flaps a piece of parchment under my nose. "Never marry! You've *ten* suitors on this list!"

She reads the names as if announcing them at a banquet, holding up each miniature in turn.

"*Gustavus Adolphus of Sweden.*"

I shake my head. "He's Protestant and will inherit the throne of Sweden. But his country is at war with Denmark, my mother's country of birth. Besides, Sweden is too far away."

"*Frederick Ulric of Brunswick-Wolfenbuttel.*"
Ann raises an eyebrow. "Hah! Can you live with
the title Wolfenbuttel? What about *Prince Maurice
of Nassau, Prince of Orange?*"

"According to my parents, he's too inferior.
According to me, he's too old! He's over forty…"

"*Theophilus, Lord Howard of Walden.*"

"According to Henry, *he's* inferior too."

"*Prince Otto of Hessia-Kassel.*"

"He speaks only German."

"*The Dauphin of France.* Now, this one would
surely make your father happy?"

"Hmm… he does fancy me queen of France,
true… And Henry says if I marry the dauphin, he
will marry the king of France's daughter so we can
be together. But now, the king of France is dead
and marriage plans have turned into funeral plans."

A sigh from Ann. She is becoming exasperated
with my excuses.

"*Victor Amadeus, son of the Duke of Savoy.*"

"Henry has had word from Sir Walter Raleigh
in the Tower that the duke has no port, and a
prince without a port cannot help us in time of

war, nor trade with us in time of peace. So, what is the point in me marrying him?"

"King Philip of Spain."

"He's a Catholic, so my mother will be happy. But, he is also recently widowed and old enough to be my father. And anyway, Henry says he is deeply stupid and on NO account must I marry a *Catholic!"*

"Prince Christian of Anhaly Bernberg."

"Also too old. He is advisor to my youngest suitor."

Then Ann makes a trumpeting noise and announces, *"And your youngest suitor is – Frederick, Elector Palatine of the Rhine!"*

"I speak no German."

She nudges me. "Look again at his portrait. With a face as handsome as his, there is no need to speak German. And they say he speaks French. He is only four days older than you and the English ambassador reports from his visit that the form of his body is perfect and he is skilful in exercise."

"The ambassador has made him sound like a horse."

"Horses don't speak French!"

I take the tiny portrait from Ann. An interesting face. Soft brown eyes. Dark eyebrows. A direct look. Perhaps this is the one.

A miniature is painted of me and sent to Frederick. I wear my hair loose around my face rather than piled high and stiff. I want him to see me as I am. I face him with a look of eagerness but not too eager – not too demure either, in a carnation silk dress trimmed in black velvet with a little lace and a single necklace.

I receive a letter from Frederick. He writes in French. He addresses me: *Ma digne princesse…* my worthy princess. He begs me to accept him. Henry approves. After lengthy discussions, so does my father. I pen a reply in French, helped by Ann.

Monsieur,

I am extremely honoured and humbled by the assurance of your friendship. I cherish it with much affection and as it is the command of the king whose

law is inviolable but whose wish I willingly obey, I am most obliged. I wait with expectancy to see you soon in these quarters.
Your very affectionate cousin,
Elizabeth

Richmond Palace, 12th September 1612

My quill hovers. "My signature should be more elaborate."

"Tie it with ribbon, stamp it with your seal and be done."

"What colour ribbon?"

"Brown – to match his dark eyes and brows."

So it happens. Four weeks later, Frederick lands at Gravesend from Germany. On a cold windswept evening in October, I hear the eighty-gun salute from the Tower announce his arrival. I stand with white knuckles, clutching Ann in the torchlit Great Chamber of Whitehall. The smell of juniper branches burning in the hearth fills the hall. My youngest brother Charles has been made to meet Frederick at the steps to the river.

I hear my father speak but I do not raise even the corner of my eye to look at Frederick as he enters. The first I see of him is the back of his dark hair as he stoops in front of me to take the hem of my garment to kiss. I sink into a deep curtsy and gather his hand to prevent it. He kisses my hand instead.

At this low level we look straight into each other's eyes. By the time he raises me, I am in love. And so, I believe, is he.

From then on Henry laughs and teases that no invitation to attend jousts, play tennis, swim the Thames, or hunt will take this man from my side.

A banquet is planned to honour Frederick. On the day, Henry's chair is empty. One of Henry's servants delivers a message that he is ill with fever. Ann looks stricken. The next day we visit him at his rooms at St James Palace. He seems cheerful. Welcomes Frederick like a brother.

Three days later, my father, on instructions from the doctor, issues orders that none may visit him.

None? Not even me – his beloved sister?

I summon Thomas and Ann. "I need coachmen who will not be recognised. I need hose, a man's doublet, a cloak, boots, a rapier and a hat to cover my hair. We will pretend to be doctor's assistants."

But no amount of disguise allows us entry to my brother's rooms. I am without news.

6TH NOVEMBER, 1612

Henry is dead. Typhoid fever.

How can it be? My dearest brother *dead*? He has been ill *one* week. It's *impossible*. I cannot bear to live. My throat is dry from sobbing. They say he called my name. Where is my sister? Why has she forsaken me?

If only he had known. I tried to visit you, my brother. I truly did!

He dies seven years, almost to the day, since the plot to kill him was uncovered. My father and mother take to their separate beds, away from Whitehall. Ann does too.

7TH DECEMBER, 1612

The longest procession I have ever seen takes Henry's body to rest in Westminster Abbey. My brother Charles leads the procession. His limp is worse than ever. The full weight of the royal crown will fall on him now. But Charles is frail and sickly. What if he does not survive my father? What if I have to wear the crown? My own black velvet train drags and weighs me down as if made of metal.

And Frederick is under scrutiny. I've heard the rumours. He might be a suitable husband for the daughter of the king of England but will he be suitable as the consort of the queen of England? Let the gossips chatter. Having lost my brother I'm not prepared to part with Frederick as well.

My father decrees the wedding *must* and *will* go ahead.

How can I mourn and celebrate at the same time? How can a wedding be held in such circumstances? But no royal wedding has taken place in England for nearly seventy years and the country is abuzz.

27TH DECEMBER,1612

Twenty days later Frederick and I are betrothed. We say our vows in French. My mother makes no appearance. Frederick wears purple velvet, laced with gold. I wear black satin with silver lace and three small white plumes in my hair. Henry's insignia. The next day the gallants at court take up the fashion in their own mourning attire.

My chambers fill with swathes of fabric, tailors, seamstresses, shoemakers and embroiderers. My favourite fabric is embroidered with birds. A shame they will be slashed to make deep pointed stomachers, tight fitting sleeves and padded shoulder pieces. I would have Mr Inigo Jones swathe it about me in Grecian style so the birds aren't harmed.

Ann and I play with the fabrics. We lift and drape and run our hands over them.

Rich ash-coloured silk grosgrain brocaded with gold and silver.

Sea-green tissued silk and tawny russet gold.

Rustling taffetas of every tincture.

Petticoats of green satin brocaded with tissued flowers.

Cobweb lawn undergarments and whalebone bodies stiffened with buckram, covered in carnation satin and crimson damask.

Buttons, ribbons, lace, tassels, from Paris and Milan.

The textures please our hands but not our hearts. The lack of Henry's presence haunts my chambers. We long for his scornful laugh to tease us away from our girlish pursuits.

My portrait is painted in sombre mood. I wear Italian silk encrusted with black pearls, a black band of mourning on my left arm. My head is set with pearls and Henry's white feathers. A heavy medallion of diamonds appears black in the painting.

St Valentine's Day, 1613

Finally the marriage day arrives. Sixteen ladies, to match my sixteen years, carry my train up the steps of Whitehall wearing silver brocade.

Ann is one of them. My hair hangs loose and long down my back, lightly plaited with pearls and diamonds. My crown is encrusted with pinnacles of diamonds and pearls, my gown is silver embroidered with silver. We are stars called down from the celestial sky.

The trumpets sound our arrival. I am strangely calm. My mother appears in public for the first time since Henry's death. My father, all in black, sits on the dais with Charles and Frederick, my beloved. Only Henry's place is empty.

Frederick is dressed in a sumptuous silver suit. The diamond I've given him as a wedding gift is pinned at his heart. He whispers, "My soul's star," as I approach. I love him more than ever.

The wedding banquet is celebrated with a lyric especially written for us by the poet, John Donne. It tells of birds. Frederick and I are two phoenixes who will kindle our love with one single flame, I am the phoenix bride who will frustrate the sun when I rise up and set the sky ablaze.

April, 1613

I stand beside Frederick again and slip my hand into his. We watch the English coast vanish. Ann is at my other side. Under my feet are the familiar boards of the *Prince Royal*. The ship built by Henry takes her maiden voyage to Europe with me aboard instead of him. On its side are his initials and his three white plumes. We sail with the royal standard of the Stuarts flying high and the figurehead of St George leading us across the ocean.

I fight back tears. Breathe in the smell of the sea. Henry's death has shrivelled my soul. But now with Frederick at my side and my hand in his, my heart breaks free. The phoenix will rise up again.

Why I Chose
Elizabeth Stuart

I grew up in a country without a king or queen, so the life of Elizabeth Stuart, daughter of a king, who was to become a queen herself, seemed like something out of a fairy tale.

I was fascinated by Elizabeth's lack of pretence – that she refused to dress formally for her portrait for Frederick, and left her hair wild and untamed. For her wedding she adopted the same fresh approach and despite the custom of the time and her mother's rigid adherence to formal dress, she wore her hair long and dishevelled down her back.

I like her playfulness and boldness – she was prepared to dress as a boy to be allowed access into her brother's rooms when he was ill. And I like her determination. It was unusual for a young princess to marry someone she truly loved.

Elizabeth almost followed the true fairytale princess format story in that, after her marriage, she went to live in a beautiful castle in Heidelberg, where Frederick built her a monkey house, an aviary, a menagerie and an Italian Renaissance garden. I visited Heidelberg Castle some years ago and wandered around those same gardens without knowing that one day I would write the story of a young girl who lived there nearly four hundred years earlier.

DIANNE HOFMEYR

Elizabeth Stuart Facts

Elizabeth Stuart was born in 1596 at Falkland Palace in Fife, Scotland. Her parents were King James VI of Scotland and Anne of Denmark. After the death of Queen Elizabeth I in 1603, Elizabeth Stuart's father became King James I of England.

On the 5th of November, 1605, an attempt to blow up the Houses of Parliament and capture Elizabeth at Coombe Abbey in Warwickshire was foiled. This date is remembered in Great Britain today as Bonfire Night.

Frederick V, Elector Palatine of the Rhine, arrived in England in October 1612 to seek Elizabeth Stuart's hand in marriage. But three weeks later, Elizabeth's beloved brother and heir to the throne, Henry Prince of Wales, died at the age of 18 from typhoid fever. The wedding was delayed and Elizabeth and Frederick finally married on Valentine's Day, 1613, at the Palace of Whitehall in London They set sail for Europe shortly afterwards, and settled at Heidelberg Castle in Germany.

In 1619, Frederick and Elizabeth were crowned King and Queen of Bohemia. They lost their titles the following year to the Holy Roman Emperor Ferdinand II, after the Battle of White Mountain, and were forced to flee to The Hague. The couple became known as the Winter King and Queen, as their reign lasted only a year.

Elizabeth died in 1662. She was survived by five of her thirteen children. Queen Elizabeth II is Elizabeth Stuart's great, great, great, great, great, great granddaughter.

A Night at the Theatre

*A story about Aphra Behn
(1640–89)*

By Marie-Louise Jensen

1677

THE HOUSE IS IN CHAOS this morning. My governess has taken to her bed with a fever on the very same morning my stepmother has gone into labour. I'm sitting playing a few lacklustre scales at the pianoforte in the drawing room, trying not to listen to the cries from the room above or the hurried footsteps of the servants on the stairs.

I'm just wishing I could be anywhere but here when the door opens and my father walks in. He looks harassed and out of place in the house at an hour when he would normally be at work.

"Jennifer, dear," he says distractedly. "Your godmother is here."

A lady follows him into the room – a tall lady in an elegant dress and with a strong, determined face which softens and breaks into a warm smile when she sees me.

"Aunt Aphra!" I cry delightedly, rushing towards my famous godmother, Mrs Aphra Behn. Her name is known throughout London, for she writes plays. It is also whispered that she was once a spy for King Charles. I adore my godmother, but my stepmother disapproves of her, so I rarely see her any more.

"Jenny," she greets me, stepping forward and kissing me on both cheeks. "My goodness, how you do resemble your dear mama!"

I blush with pleasure. Mama died three years ago. I loved her dearly and am proud to look like her.

"We thought, my dear," my father explains, "that you might like to go and stay with your godmother for a day or so. Just until—" He winces as a particularly loud cry comes down through the ceiling.

I practically dance for joy.

"Run up and help the maid pack your bag, Jennifer," my father instructs me. "Be sure to pack some warm clothes and... er... whatever you need for the night."

After that, it is all bustle and frantic preparations until I'm standing in the street, being handed in to a hackney carriage. My father presses some money into my hand at the last minute and bids me be a good girl and enjoy myself.

The coach is rattling down the street before I have a chance to turn to my godmother. Her eyes are sparkling with mischief. "I've finally got you to myself, my dear Jenny!" she says gleefully. "Your stepmother is so horrified by my involvement in the theatre that I almost despaired of ever seeing you again. She is terrified her friends will discover such a shocking connection."

My stepmother is very religious.

"She calls the theatre a haunt of vice," I confide. "And a den of wickedness."

Aunt Aphra throws her head back and laughs out loud, making me giggle too. "I can just hear her saying it," she says. "By the way, Jenny, speaking of the theatre... I just *happen* to have a new play being performed for the very first time today. I didn't think it was right to mention it to your papa, for he has so much on his mind just now. But should you object very much to accompanying me this afternoon to see it performed?"

I gasp. A fizz of excitement rushes through me.

"Truly?" I demand, awed by the prospect.

"Yes, truly, child," says Aunt Aphra, leaning forward and patting me on the cheek. "Is that a big enough treat?"

"Oh – the very best!" I say. I really mean it. All my life I've dreamed of going to the theatre. When my mother was alive, I was too young. Now I'm thirteen and have been old enough for *ages*.

We stop at my aunt's lodging to drop off my bag and then we set out for the theatre on foot. On the way, I see playbills posted here and there, announcing THE ROVER: *A New Play by Mrs Behn performing today at the Theatre Royal.*

"What's the play about?" I ask eagerly.

"It's about a young girl like you," Aunt Aphra tells me. "But she doesn't love the old man she is ordered to marry. So she determines to go out into the city in a mask and see something of life before she is wed."

I stop in the middle of the pavement and clasp my hands together in excitement. My aunt laughs, takes me by the elbow and draws me on beside her.

"Come, Jenny, you will block up the street!"

"Does she have adventures?" I ask. "Does she... fall in love?"

"Of course. With a rover, a handsome traveller, as the title promises. But I'll tell you no more. You'll have to wait and see what befalls the fair Helena."

The Theatre Royal is a big, imposing building in Drury Lane. As we enter, we are immediately jostled by a crowd of people. It is all very grand and fine. Aunt Aphra leads me through a door marked *Private* and along a corridor. We are 'backstage' now, she tells me, and here everything is much plainer.

"I'll show you around," she says, opening another door, and we enter the theatre itself. "And this, my dear Jenny, is where it all happens!" I look around me in amazement. The theatre is so much larger than anything I'd imagined. The stage itself is huge and slopes down towards where the audience sit.

"The area in front of the stage where the benches are set out is called the pit," my godmother explains. At the back of the auditorium are the tiers of galleries. On either side are the boxes. "That one is the royal box." She points at the largest and grandest of them.

I gaze around. "And why are so many people here already? Surely the play is not about to start already?"

"No, the play begins at four thirty. But many people come before that to see their friends and chat."

"I see and... oh! Who is that lady in the mask? Is she one of the actresses?" I point to a woman in a low-cut dress and a face mask that reveals only her eyes, who is walking among the men in the pit.

"No, she... To tell the truth, Jenny, she is one of the reasons your stepmother disapproves of the theatre. You don't need to know about her. Come backstage instead! There is a great deal to see!"

Aunt Aphra leads me through more corridors, showing me offices, storerooms, props and then to a large room where a number of women are applying cosmetics and having their hair dressed.

There's a crowd of people around them, laughing and talking to them. I can see grand costumes hanging up, ready to be put on for the performance.

"Who are all these other people?" I ask. "Will they all be in the play too?"

"No, my dear. These are favoured guests, invited in to watch the actresses prepare themselves for the stage. It's a sociable place, the theatre."

We pause and watch one actress being laced into her gown. She looks very fine indeed.

The men's changing room is much less crowded. To my amazement, the men, in their breeches and loose shirts, are painting their faces just as the ladies were. I blush to intrude upon them, but they all greet my godmother with great friendliness. "Have you come to make sure we are dressed on time, Mrs Behn?" asks one older gentleman. "Or to check we haven't forgotten the fine lines you've written for us?" He smiles but I'm a little frightened of him. The make-up he wears on his face looks grotesque up close – thick and bright.

"To reassure myself that you are all prepared and in good cheer," replies Aunt Aphra with a smile.

We pause to exchange a few words here and there, one of the men blows Aunt Aphra a kiss, calls her lovely lady, and we move on.

We've barely emerged from the men's changing rooms (to my relief – I've a strong feeling my stepmother *definitely* wouldn't approve of *that* visit) when a man comes rushing up to my godmother.

"Mrs Behn," he cries. "Thank heavens you are here! We have an emergency."

There's a hurried, whispered conference between them while I politely try to look as though I'm not listening.

"Oh dear," says Aunt Aphra at last, turning to me. "I'm afraid I need to go and sort a few things out, Jenny. Now, what should you..." She frowns, but just then a boy about my own age passes down the corridor and my godmother's face brightens. "Peter!" she says. "You'll look after my goddaughter for me for a short time, won't you?"

The boy's cheerful face falls. "But I'm just about to light lamps and check the scenes," he protests.

"Oh, can I not stay with you, Aunt Aphra?" I beg.

She laughs her merry laugh. "No, Jenny, you cannot. This is a delicate matter. And, Peter, Jennifer can help you."

She disappears in a swirl of petticoats. Peter and I look at each other awkwardly in the narrow corridor. "Well then, we'd better make the best of this," says Peter and I'm relieved to see his freckled face turn cheerful once more. "I'm Peter," he says, thrusting out a grubby hand.

"I'm Jenny," I respond, shaking his hand gingerly.

I follow him to a storeroom, where he fetches a couple of tapers. He lights them at a lamp, then we go out on to the actual stage. I'm very aware of being on view before a half-full theatre, but most people are too busy talking to pay us any attention. A man called Alfred lowers the chandeliers over the stage, one at a time, so that we can light them. We use both tapers, lighting the candles between us as quickly as we can so that they can be hoisted into place again.

"Do you work here all the time?" I ask Peter curiously.

"I do. I live here too," he says proudly. "My ma was an actress but she died when I were just a lad, so they took me in here."

"Oh my mama is dead too," I tell him sympathetically. "I miss her very much."

"Ah, but you'll have a pa still. And Mrs Behn is your godmama. She's a fine lady. Always has a kind word."

"Yes, indeed, I love them both very much. Is your papa dead too?"

Peter shrugged. "Might be for all I know," he says. "Come on, we're done here. Let's go and check the scenes."

The theatre is bustling now; the pit is thronged with gentlemen in colourful clothes talking and walking about. A sprinkling of finely dressed ladies have joined them. The boxes too, are filling up with people drinking tea or sipping wine and talking. Fruit sellers walk around, loudly shouting out their wares.

I follow Peter behind the curtain, which is drawn before the great arch above the stage, and I'm amazed at the sight of the complex machinery that moves the different backdrops of scenery and screens around.

"See here," Peter points out a screen that is set in a groove in the floor. "I pull this rope here to pull this screen to one side, just at the right moment, and then – hey presto! A new scene is revealed behind!"

"I'm so envious of you working here!" I say with a happy sigh, duly admiring the wonderful mechanism. "Do you love it?"

"It's the best work there is, I reckon," Peter says with a grin. "And the best people and all."

"When I'm older," I say resolutely, "I will ask Aunt Aphra to find me work in the theatre! *Whatever* my stepmother has to say about it."

"Bet you won't," says Peter. He darts away, beckoning me. I climb some stairs after him and then follow him up a steep ladder. "Are we allowed to be here?" I ask breathlessly as we reach the top. We're very high, right up in the roof space above the stage. From here we can see the whole stage laid out below and the front of the pit too.

Peter points to the pit. "You'll marry one of

those fine gentlemen there, I reckon," he says. "And won't never come near the theatre except maybe to see the play now and then."

I look down soberly. "I don't care about marrying," I say. "I would far rather work in the theatre!"

Peter shows me the way back to my godmother's box just before the performance begins and says goodbye. Aunt Aphra is bowing to all her acquaintances around the theatre, but goes quite still when suddenly the door of the royal box on the opposite side of the theatre opens and King Charles himself walks in. Aunt Aphra drops at once into a deep curtsey and pulls me down into a less elegant one beside her.

"Your deepest curtsey for royalty, Jenny," she says under her breath. "Head down too, don't stare."

I obey her, but whisper back: "Mama always told me you were angry with the king, Aunt Aphra?"

"When I was his spy and he failed to pay me, and I was thrown into a debtor's prison," admits my godmother, rising slowly from her curtsey as the king sits down. "But when he honours the first night of my new play with his presence, I could kiss his feet. I'm the most loyal subject in his kingdom."

"A spy!" I say with a sigh. "How romantic! Not being thrown into prison, of course! But it must have been such an adventure! Wasn't that *even* more exciting than working in the theatre?"

"Oh, yes," my godmother agrees. "But there is nothing like being paid for the work you do!"

The king notices Aunt Aphra and gives her a small bow. The king – *the king of England!* – has come to see my godmother's play! I'm so proud of her, I could burst.

But now someone is on the stage, ready to speak. I hurriedly scramble into my seat and settle down to watch. The orange seller stops her endless cries and the man on stage begins to deliver the prologue. I hold my breath with excitement. My first play!

But not everyone is as excited as me, it seems. Many of them don't even bother to stop speaking, and there are three young men on the stage, actually sitting *right on the stage*, booing the speaker off and calling for the dancing girls and the actresses.

I look at my godmother to see how she takes this, but apart from some mild irritation she seems quite calm.

When the prologue has been spoken, the curtain rises and in just a few moments, I'm deeply engrossed in the story. The spectacle of actors and actresses on the stage, the singing and the dancing all dazzle me. I understand now why they were so heavily painted. From a distance their faces look just right.

The only problem is the chatter, laughter, flirting and quarrelling going on in the pit, which makes the beautiful speeches so difficult to hear. "Are they never quiet?" I ask my aunt in the interval.

"Never!" she says with a sigh. "The king greatly dislikes the disorder in the theatre. He objects to the bucks on stage ogling the dancing girls too. I wouldn't be surprised if he has them moved before the next act."

At that moment, my godmother is summoned to speak to the king. She beckons me to follow her. "Oh no, I would so much rather stay here," I protest, but she shakes her head, takes my hand and leads me after her.

I'm so overwhelmed to be in the presence of the king that I can barely breathe while he speaks to my aunt. "Another fine play, Mrs Behn," he says. "Congratulations! I look forward to the next two acts. And who is this young lady?"

"Your Majesty, may I introduce my goddaughter, Miss Richards?"

I curtsey deeply again. I'm shaking as I straighten up.

"How do you like the theatre, Miss Richards?" the king asks me.

"Oh! I love it. Um... Your Majesty!" I say, flustered.

The king laughs. "So do we. So do we. But we must have those men off the stage. See to it," he orders one of his attendants.

Our audience with the king over, we return to our box. I'm flushed with excitement and sit in a daze as the actors return to the stage and resume the tale.

The second half of the play is as enthralling as the first and without members of the audience on the stage, it is easier to concentrate. The second half is interrupted, however, by a fight breaking out in the pit. Two gentlemen quarrel, get their swords out and fight, while the other visitors scream and try to get away from the lethal blades.

"Oh, Aunt Aphra!" I exclaim fearfully, clinging to her hand. "Will someone be killed?"

"I hope not, Jenny," she says, wincing at a particularly wicked thrust. But the king's men break the fight up swiftly and the play resumes. I'm so happy when Helena marries the rover at the end that I cry.

The epilogue is spoken. People stand to clap and stamp their feet, cheering and shouting while the actors take their bows. The king claps too and looks approving.

I sit quite still in my seat as the curtain finally falls, not wanting to move and break the enchantment. "Congratulations, Aunt Aphra,"

I whisper at last, as the applause dies and people begin to talk and move about again. "Is it very wonderful to see the words you have written performed?"

"Always, Jenny," she says, cheeks aglow and eyes sparkling. "And I think we can safely say it was a success!"

At that moment, there is a knock at the door of our box. It's Peter. "Note for you, Mrs Behn," he says. "It come from your lodging just now and they said it was urgent."

Aunt Aphra opens the crackling sheet and reads it swiftly, looking up with a smile. "Why, Jenny," she said. "Wonderful news! We must congratulate you too: you have a baby brother!"

I experience a jolt of shock and then a rush of excitement. A real baby – a brother!

"I suggest you stay with me tonight as we agreed," says my godmother. "You can return home in the morning. Now we should celebrate the success of the play *and* the birth of your brother, shouldn't we?"

"Oh, yes please, Aunt Aphra!" I tell my

godmother eagerly. "This has been the best night of my life! I want to work in the theatre like you one day!"

Aphra Behn smiles. "If that's what you want to do, I hope you will, Jenny," she says. "There will be those who oppose your wishes. But remember: only you can decide how you will spend your life. Make your own decisions and if I can help you, I will."

Why I Chose Aphra Behn

I chose to write about Aphra Behn because she did so much to blaze the writing trail for the many women who followed her. She lived in Africa for a spell, was a spy for King Charles II, and became the first woman known to have made a living writing in the English language. She started writing originally to get herself out of a debtor's prison. I love her plays, particularly *The Rover*, which continued to be performed for 100 years. She also wrote an early novel, *Oroonoko*. She was a woman ahead of her time.

I invented Jenny and her family to show how Aphra Behn inspired many other women to lead independent lives and to write for the theatre as she did.

MARIE-LOUISE JENSEN

Aphra Behn Facts

Aphra Behn was born Aphra Johnson, probably in Canterbury, in 1640. She is thought to have lived in Surinam, West Africa from 1663–64 and to have married a Mr Behn shortly after returning to England. He supposedly died the following year but no records of such a person have survived. It's possible she invented the marriage to give herself a respectable social status as a widow. Aphra was a spy for King Charles II from 1666–67, under the code name *Astrea*, but he didn't pay her and she was thrown into a debtor's prison. She wrote poems and stories to get herself out of debt. She also wrote many plays, of which *The Rover* was the most successful.

Aphra Behn died in 1689 and is buried in Westminster Abbey. The twentieth-century writer Virginia Woolf said of her in *A Room of One's Own:*

'All women together ought to let flowers fall upon the tomb of Aphra Behn, [...] for it was she who earned them the right to speak their minds.'

An Unimportant Woman

*A story about Mary Wollstonecraft
(1759–1797)*

BY PENNY DOLAN

NEAR TONSBERG, NORWAY, 1795

I WALKED THROUGH THE SILENT ROOMS, remembering my father, until my aunt Solveig came to claim me.

"Time to go, Anna. The new pastor's carriage is arriving soon." She patted my arm. "All is arranged. You will come with me to the count's mansion at Jarlsberg."

My aunt was the count's housekeeper and a good and respectable woman. I told myself I should be grateful. Besides, where else could I go?

One week before, the day after my fourteenth birthday, the old pastor – my father – was buried. I took three roses to the churchyard. One was for Father, one for my mother, gone two years before, and one for my brother's grave. Never had I felt so alone.

After the funeral, I was called before the clerk of the parish. He set aside his stack of papers and explained how things stood.

"Prepare yourself, child. It seems that your father – God rest his soul – did not understand much about money."

I asked, I did. "Father spoke of an inheritance from my grandfather?"

The clerk was not pleased. "Spent already, on your brother's education."

And, I thought, *on paying off my brother's debts, and on the horse that broke my brother's handsome neck.*

The clerk bent his head to pray. Could he hear the thoughts shouting in my head?

Oh, Father, did you not bother about me for one minute? Is a daughter nothing at all? How, in heaven's name, am I to live? On good folk's charity?

Apart from a Bible and a few trinkets, there was almost nothing left.

The clerk muttered about God's will but all I felt was anger. My father, the good pastor, had left me homeless, helpless and penniless. I think the English have a saying: 'as poor as a church mouse'. That poor mouse was me.

So it was that Aunt Solveig brought me to live with her at the count's fine house.

The manor had forty large windows. They stared across the count's lawns, right down to the sea's edge. They watched the great ships sailing north to Christiana, east to Sweden or south to our king in Denmark. Some were on course for the war-troubled English Channel and beyond.

The count never saw his view. Our king sent him to be the royal ambassador at the court of King George in London. Such an important gentleman was too busy to visit his manor house, especially when he had grander homes elsewhere.

So why were my aunt and all the others there? They were there to watch and wait, to keep the manor ready, *in case* the count ever decided to visit.

My aunt, the aged butler and the house servants looked after the manor inside. The count's agent and his men looked after the outside, the wide grounds and the small harbour beyond.

My aunt's room was not fine. It was tucked away at the back of the house. There was just enough room for my small wooden trunk and I had to share Aunt Solveig's feather bed. Each night, when her snoring woke me, I lay there in the dark, wondering what would become of me.

My aunt made one thing clear.

"Anna," she told me, "a pastor's daughter cannot be a servant or maid. You would shame your father's name. And mine. I will tell you what you can and cannot do."

So I lived in the shadow of my aunt. I tried to hide my discontent but I stabbed my needle when I reworked old embroideries. I stamped down the empty stone passages when I delivered messages. I scowled to myself when I filled the flower vases.

I was kept busy but what was I? Companion? Secretary? What was my purpose?

If the count ever visits, I decided, *perhaps he will be able to tell me.*

But he wasn't the one who helped me. It was the unimportant woman – for that is what my aunt called her – and she came as a summer visitor.

Visits happened like this: gentlefolk wrote, asking to see the count's house and his treasures. Often, they hoped he would be in residence.

As each request arrived, Aunt Solveig noted the day in the diary. Then she would hand the envelope to me. My task, as her helper, was to copy out a neat reply, adding the correct names and dates, of course.

"You have such beautiful handwriting, child," she would tell me, rubbing her swollen fingers. "Your mother taught you well."

Visitors meant more work. Before anyone arrived, the house servants had to remove the sheets from the best statues and dust the picture frames. They would roll back the covers on the expensive carpets, so the patterns could be seen. Then my aunt would send me from room to room strewing scented herbs to sweeten the air and drive away any fleas.

Usually, my aunt guided the visitors around, wearing her best dress and silver brooch. She would show them the important objects, answering questions when she could, and telling polite tales.

And, usually, I was kept at her side, in my one good dress – plain, with a neat lace-edged collar. I opened doors. I closed doors. I poured out the refreshment when required. I smiled prettily and would curtsey now and again. Such manners were important. If we pleased the visitors, they slid coins into Aunt Solveig's aching, lace-mittened hands.

The woman's request arrived at Midsummer, when Scandinavian nights are almost as light as day and Aunt Solveig slept badly.

"A single visitor is hardly worth the bother," she snapped, fanning her face with the envelope. "Who is this Mrs Mary Imlay? I have not heard her name."

I scanned the letter. "She says she is a writer. A journalist."

"Anna, how can a woman be such a thing? What would she have to say? Who would listen? Perhaps the writer is a man she is bringing with her? Show me."

Aunt Solveig turned the sheet over but there was no post-script. She pursed her lips, displeased.

So, on the day the unimportant woman was due, my aunt had already decided. "Anna, you will be Mrs Imlay's guide today," she told me. "I'm sure you know what to say and do." She sighed dramatically. "I am feeling rather out of sorts."

I waited, ready. The carriage wheels crunched on the gravel outside and the footman opened the door. Mrs Imlay walked through, handing him her travelling cloak. She was alone.

Immediately, she looked around the hall with great curiosity. She scribbled words down in a small notebook. I had thought only gentlemen did that.

"Welcome, madam." The words felt strange in my mouth.

Mrs Imlay had a strange energy about her. She was not truly beautiful and she was no longer young, although her hair was glossy and her eyes dark and striking. Her dress was severe enough for a church service and she held herself most proudly.

I explained as best I could. "The housekeeper

is unwell, madam, although there is no infection and no cause for alarm. She sends her apologies and has instructed me to guide you, if you please."

"Instructed *you*, has she? Almost a child?" the woman said, vexed.

I bit my lip nervously. Then her manner softened. For a moment she stared at me so intently that I blushed.

"Perhaps it *will* please me," she said with a smile. "There is intelligence in your face." She spoke in French, which my mother had taught me, but she was English. "Your name?"

"Anna."

"And you are…?"

"The housekeeper's niece," I said. "My parents are dead."

"So you are a girl alone?" She narrowed her eyes and studied me. "Maybe your father believed you were a beauty? Maybe he expected you to marry well?"

I shook my head. "No. I was to stay at home and look after him."

She sniffed. "In my opinion, fathers rarely see

the true value of their daughters," she commented coldly. Then she gave a shrug. "On the other hand, some girls cannot help being a burden, as my sisters showed me."

I kept silent. I was supposed to be talking about statues, not opinions on sisters.

"Come, Anna, what's through here?" she said, leading me into the long half-lit corridor.

Around the walls, among ancient weapons, hung the hunting trophies. The heads of animals – bears, wild boars, badgers, huge antlered deer – all killed for sport. Their glass eyes glittered in the candlelight.

The woman stopped, shuddered and put her hand to her heart.

"Madam, are you well?" I asked.

"Well enough." Taking a breath, she nodded. "I cannot admire those trophies, child."

I was puzzled. The tour was not supposed to go like this. Now I should be pointing out the great bear that nearly killed the count's father.

But she had already continued. "For the last few years, I have been living in Paris—"

I gasped. I couldn't help it. "Paris? Where the people killed the king?"

"Yes, Anna. Paris." Her eyes blazed with passion. "Believe me, the people rose in good faith, in the name of freedom and liberty. Reason was on their side but the king and his court would not listen."

She turned away from the stuffed heads above.

"Then trouble and terror did come. Heads, bad and good, began to roll from the guillotine. That I cannot forget."

"You saw that?" I was ashamed to sound so curious. "The deaths? The riots?"

"Would you seek out such sights, child? No. I lived as quietly as I could. I wrote. I saw a few friends."

"And your husband, Mr Imlay?"

She paused, brow furrowed "Ah! *Mr Imlay, the American adventurer, abiding in London!* The French believe all Americans are their brothers, fighting the English lion for independence. Mr Imlay's nationality protects me," she said, smiling grimly, "but I am still Mary Wollstonecraft."

Suddenly she reached inside her dress and drew out a locket on a long chain. "Look!"

Inside, for me to admire, was a sketch of a one-year-old child. "My daughter is waiting at Gothenburg with her nurse," she said and sighed. "How I miss the little creature!"

Then off she went again, walking briskly to the gallery. I trotted alongside, guiding her towards the watercolours of the house and the small harbour.

"Will the count develop the area?" she asked. "I saw the king's salt-works along the coast. This is such an admirable country."

She turned, and seeing the large painting opposite, almost pushed past me to admire it.

It was a wild landscape. Torrents cascaded down the mountainsides, storm clouds brooded around rocky precipices but, high in the sky, was a glorious sun.

"Oh, Anna, what joy! I am so fond of such images. The sublime and the picturesque! Ah, men lock the world's Great Power away inside churches and cathedrals and prayer books. It is all around us, if we only look."

I was glad my aunt had not heard such blasphemous words. She might have died from shock.

"The family portraits are worth seeing, Mrs Imlay. Over here," I said, anxiously.

She laughed softly at the count and his family, dressed in their finest silks and brocades.

"Why do these men always behave so importantly? And must all women be taught to simper so stupidly? What do you think, Anna? Should a woman act like a lapdog?"

I did not know what I thought. But I did know that my heart was beating fast and that my mind was echoing with her words.

She did not wait for an answer. She strode off again. "This must be the count's library? May I see?"

I pushed open the double doors. She entered. I waited outside in the corridor, as Aunt Solveig does.

Mrs Imlay turned, surprised. "Come in too, child!"

I took three steps forward, on to the carpet.

"Have you not been inside here before?"

I shook my head. "No."

"But you can read? Your father taught you that at least?"

"Of course. He taught me to copy out his sermons too—"

Swiftly she seized my hands and looked hard into my eyes. I was alarmed. Visitors did not behave like this.

"*Copy?* Anna, copying makes a good beginning but a girl like you could write her own words. Why not write what you think about? Or what you discover?"

I was unable to answer.

"Sit," she ordered, patting the chaise longue. I perched beside her. "You see these books?" She pointed along the shelves.

"Yes." There were rows and rows.

"Read them, Anna. If a girl is not given an education then she must get one for herself. Learn how people think. Learn to think yourself. Learn about how people live, and how they should live as rational, sensible equals, women as well as men. That will be the new world."

How can I explain this moment? When the woman spoke, it was as if she were on fire. I leaned back, afraid of being burned by her energy.

"Anna, there are so many new ideas in the world just now. Papers, pamphlets... You must search. You must take hold of these new times and not be afraid. Nations are asking for independence everywhere – America, France, Ireland. Even back in England. Independence is the spirit of the future. And you, Anna, must make something better of yourself, not just as spinster, wife or widow. It is hard, but it *is* possible!"

Then, as she stopped for breath, her mood changed. A deep sadness filled her eyes.

"Do you need some refreshment, Mrs Imlay?" I said gently. "There is a tray in the hall."

"Thank you," she said. Her voice was hardly more than a whisper.

She set her glass back on the tray, smiling ruefully. "Anna, you must excuse me. Sometimes I am too passionate in my feelings. It causes trouble –

I know it – even when what I am saying is right."

In the quiet, a far-off church bell rang.

She sighed deeply. "I am weary, Anna. I've travelled up and down the coast, meeting this official or that official. I am on a quest, searching for the ship that holds Mr Imlay's cargo of silver, and it is hard."

For a moment, I wondered why Mr Imlay had not come himself. Then I remembered how my brother had behaved. Money slips like water through some men's hands.

Then she hit her knee with her fist. "The clerks in the shipping offices don't expect to answer a woman's questions, but I persevere. I show them how determined I am. Every time."

She rose and asked me for her travelling cloak. "Anna, this afternoon has been a rest and a pleasure. Thank you." And then she was gone.

I handed the coins to my aunt. But the woman had given me something for my own, too. Before leaving, she had pressed a small book into my hands.

"Begin your own education, Anna," she had told me.

"I hope that woman hasn't been putting ideas into your head," my aunt commented.

That was exactly what the woman had done. The book was called *A Vindication of the Rights of Women*. Her own name was printed inside: *Mary Wollstonecraft*.

I do not think she was unimportant.

Why I Chose
Mary Wollstonecraft

I chose Mary because she called for girls to be well-educated, for men and women to live as equal partners, and for the rights of both men and women in an age when only a few men had the power to vote.

I also admire Mary because, unlike many famous women, she was not aristocratic or wealthy. She came from a troubled, unsettled family. At a time when prettiness and wealth were essential for 'a good marriage', Mary had little fortune or great beauty. However, she was incredibly determined: given little formal schooling, she educated herself, gaining a reputation as an outspoken writer, intellectual and journalist. Even so, Mary's headstrong, passionate personality did not make her life easy, happy or long.

I based this story on a visit mentioned in Mary's published letters about a trip to Scandinavia, trying to imagine how a young girl might feel on meeting the remarkable Mary at a certain moment in her own life.

PENNY DOLAN

Mary Wollstonecraft Facts

Mary Wollstonecraft was born in Spitalfields, London, in 1759. She was the second of seven children. Her mother neglected her, and her father was violent and reckless with money.

In 1784, Mary set up a school in Islington, London, with her two sisters and best friend, Fanny Blood, but it did not succeed. Two years later, in 1786, Mary went to Ireland to work as governess to Lord and Lady Kingsborough's children. She was dismissed after just a year, for being too strong an influence on the two daughters.

On her return to London, Mary began writing for the printer Joseph Johnson. He was the publisher of a radical magazine, the *Analytical Review*, and during this time, Mary met many free thinkers and reformers.

In 1790, Mary wrote *A Vindication of the Rights of Man* in which she attacked the power of the aristocracy and supported republican ideals. This was followed in 1792 by her most famous book, *A Vindication of the Rights of Women*.

The same year, Mary set off alone to live in Paris, France, so that she could write about the new republic. Just three years before, the downtrodden people had stormed the Bastille prison, beginning the French Revolution. There, in 1793, while France and England were at war, Mary met Gilbert Imlay, an American adventurer. She registered as his wife at the American Embassy in September of the same year. By October 1793, with one revolutionary party dominating, the 'Terror' began, a period of extreme violence during which tens of thousands of 'enemies of the Revolution' were executed. English people were arrested too, but as Imlay's registered wife, Mary was safe, and had her first baby, Fanny, in 1794.

Soon after, Imlay left for England. In 1795, Mary followed him but he did not want any reunion. Nevertheless, that June, on behalf of Imlay's business, Mary sailed to Scandinavia. Her letters home, describing these travels, were published a year later. Imlay soon disappeared, leaving Mary and his daughter and perhaps returning to America.

In 1797, in London, Mary was officially married to a philosopher, William Godwin. That August, Mary gave birth to her second daughter, who became famous as Mary Shelley, the author of the novel *Frankenstein*.

Sadly, Mary Wollstonecraft died soon after her daughter's birth, on 10th September 1797. Her life had been dramatic, unconventional and bold.

Best After Storms

*A story of Mary Anning
(1799–1847)*

BY JOAN LENNON

Outside the window, lightning ripped across the blackness of the night. Thunder battered their ears, and when it faded, they could hear the roaring of the ocean, flinging itself hungrily at the cliffs.

Peggy trembled, thinking thoughts of peril on the sea, but Mrs Lark paid no attention. She was a local woman, and used to storms. Her hands were steady as she shielded the candle flame and bent down to check on the figure lying so still in the bed.

"Do you think she's frightened?" whispered Peggy.

Peggy's real name was Margaret, but nobody called her that. She'd lately come to Lyme Regis and was learning how to be a nurse. Mrs Lark said she'd do well enough once she stopped being so fanciful. But it was hard, trying not to imagine herself in the place of every patient.

"Frightened of a storm?" said Mrs Lark. "Mary Anning? Not a bit of it. Look – she's smiling."

Peggy looked, and it was true. The sick woman in the bed had the sweetest smile on her face.

What do you suppose she's thinking about? Peggy wondered but, reminding herself to act like a proper nurse, she didn't say it out loud.

— ❄ —

Of course I'm not frightened of a storm! I've lived my whole life within the sound of the sea. I remember so many wild nights, over the years – and one in particular.

Such a storm that was! I'd been awake for hours, wondering what was being washed away while I was stuck in my bed, waiting for the daylight to come and the wind to drop. Sometimes the waves would batter the coast for days and you would get to the point where you'd give anything for a bit of peace. The wailing of the wind could get to sound like nails on slate or mad people, rattling the windows and trying to get in.

"Please don't be a storm like that," I whispered to the darkness.

And, for a wonder, it wasn't! The morning came, washed clean, with a blue sky and flying white clouds and a salt sea tang in the air. Perfect for hunting monsters.

It's always best after storms.

But first there were the chores. I riddled the fire, brought in fresh coal, water from the pump. The chickens never liked it when the wind was up, but Belinda the old brown hen always obliged. I was in such a hurry I almost dropped her warm speckled egg on to the cobblestones. Caught it just in time!

My dear dog Tray was excited too. He pressed himself up against my leg as I laid out the breakfast things and I could feel his warm little body trembling.

"Soon, boy. Chores almost done and then, we'll go. I promise!"

A weak voice called down from upstairs, "Mary? Bring me back some laudanum from the shop before you go to the shore. Will you? There's a good girl…"

Tray whimpered. I sighed.

"Never mind," I told him. "We'll run the whole way."

But of course we didn't. Too many eyes watching. Too many wagging tongues and judging frowns. Running wasn't proper behaviour for a girl. Neither was hunting monsters!

As I came into Mr Lloyd's shop I was glad I'd walked so demurely, for I saw that Mrs Crouch was there, talking to a stranger. Mrs Crouch was the worst gossip in a town full of gossips. She had such an edge to her tongue it's a miracle she didn't cut her own mouth. I did my best to school my face.

"A penny's worth of laudanum, and put it on the slate, if you please, Mr Lloyd," I said.

And then I just had to stand there and wait for him to slowly, carefully, measure out the medicine.

Mrs Crouch rents out her upstairs rooms to poorly souls sent to Lyme Regis for the bracing sea air. Even if she didn't need the income, I think she would have them anyway – a never-ending audience for her tale-telling and slanders.

I could hear her whispering about me now.

"That's Mary Anning, you know. She was hit by lightning when she was a baby. It killed three women standing there – including the one holding her! – but didn't damage a hair of her head. Was the making of her, in fact, for I remember what a scrawny hopeless little scrap she was before it happened and afterwards she was as pink and round as a healthy piglet!"

A piglet? Thank you VERY much!

Whisper, whisper.

"Well, they *do* say she can see things that other folk can't... No, not like a witch. I'm quite sure... Bones. Not people's bones, no..."

Mutter, murmur.

"Well, I'm a God-fearing woman. You'll not find anyone who'll tell you any different. But they do say..."

I didn't need to be hearing the rest. Nobody tells anyone they're God-fearing unless they're meaning that someone else *isn't*.

Did the stranger pull her skirts aside ever so slightly as I left?

"Who cares, eh, Tray?" I whispered, bending down to stroke his head.

So I see things other folk don't – I *see* the

bones I find - I don't *conjure* them! Do they think I'm out in the dark clambering about the cliffs and along the shore putting the beasts into the rocks? My beautiful monsters – do they think they're all witchcraft and magic? This is the nineteenth century, for pity's sake!

Don't think about it, I tell myself so many times a day. *Don't think about the illness at home, or the worry about the rent, or even where the penny for the laudanum is supposed to come from.* These are thoughts to be pushed behind doors in my mind, especially with the shore calling.

I ran indoors, put the bottle within reach and then we were off! We left behind the town and the watchers and the stale, sad smell of the sick room. The shore stretched away and there was no one judging me here so I let my bonnet hang by its strings down my back – the wind could do what it liked with my hair. I hitched up my skirts and jumped from stone to shingle to sand to stone in my tackety boots, hunting along the low tide line. Tray rushed ahead and then back to me a dozen times a minute, his ears flapping like sails in the wind and a smile of pure delight all over his dear face.

If I'd found nothing at all it would still have been a joy just to be there, but the storm had left gifts for me beyond the salt tang in the air and the clean spray against my face. I spotted a stone of just the right shape – I cradled it in my hand and tapped it with my hammer, so that it split perfectly to reveal the fossil of an ammonite.

I'd found bigger specimens before, but this one was so beautifully complete. Not very long ago, people still believed they were serpent stones – coiled snakes petrified by some saint or other. They used to carve snake heads on to them to up the price.

"You're a beauty," I told the ammonite. "You'll fetch a pretty penny just as you are." Which made me think about all the pennies' worth of debt on Mr Lloyd's slate. *No! I won't think about that. Not here. Not now.*

I was vaguely aware of Tray barking and a flock of gulls taking off, sending flying shadows across the shore. I took a few more taps at the ammonite with my hammer but then decided to stow it in my basket instead. It was a job to do carefully, at home.

The rumble took me by surprise.

Stupidly, I looked out to sea, thinking there must be some sudden, savage wave smashing into the shore. I stared, reaching my hand down to Tray to grab him by the scruff in case we needed to make a run for it...

He wasn't there. He wasn't there! The rumble was *behind* me, from landward, and now it was a roar. I spun round as the beach ruckled itself under my feet and the scattered pools shivered – and then I saw it. A river of rock, sliding down the side of the cliff and across the flat surface of the shore on its way to the sea and, just ahead of its leading edge, streaking towards me in a blur of black and white fur, was my Tray.

Save yourself, Mary! something screamed in my head, but my legs would not bend.

"Tray... Tray!" And then he was in my arms and I staggered back into the white foam at the edge of the water. I squeezed my eyes tight shut.

For a long moment I don't think either of us breathed – until a wave came crashing in, drenching my legs in icy water, and I opened my eyes with a yelp.

The slide had stopped, just at the sea's edge. The scree had pooled almost at my feet. And a whole new segment of cliff face was visible.

Of course the sensible thing to do then would have been to splash through the shallows, back towards the town, carefully skirting the debris for fear of starting another slide. I considered doing just that. But the raw new limestone surface drew me like a moth to a candle.

"Always best after storms," I murmured, setting Tray down. "Gently does it."

We crept forward, slithering a little where the scree was still loose. It was all I could do to stop staring at the cliff face and pay attention to where I was putting my feet. How long had that rock been hidden from the sky? That rock and all it contained...

Closer and closer, trying not to stumble, the danger growing greater with every step. A sudden gust of wind or a gull landing at the top of the cliff could bring it all down on our heads. *This is mad, Mary – you should stop now – you should go back, quiet as a mouse... You really should –*

And there it was. Looking at me out of the stone, its unblinking eye fixed on me, as if in astonishment.

"What – have you never seen a girl before?" I asked it. "I thought dragons ate girls!"

Not that I thought for a moment this *was* a dragon. It was something much more exciting than that.

Tray whined and I stroked his soft ears. In all honesty, I was calming myself as much as I was calming him. I had to be sure it wasn't just my eyes playing tricks on me. Not just wishful thinking.

"Gently does it, lad. Gently does it. Nothing to worry about." I looked into Tray's loving eyes, drew his silken ears through my fingers one more time and straightened up.

The great skull was clearly visible, poking out of the limestone. And, as I had hoped, I could see where there was more.

Take a breath, Mary, I told myself. *Take a breath...*

I could see where the entire body of the creature stretched out beneath a thin layer of stone – spine, limbs, tail – each bone was there to be brought clear of the encasing rock and into the light. Carefully, though. Oh so carefully. I could see it even before I'd hit a single blow with my hammer – the shape in the rock, like a body under a sheet. Something from the deep time, long ago, when this great beast and the others like him were as common as cart horses and cows are today.

I gathered Tray up and hugged his warm little squirmy body tight in my arms and let him lick my face. "We've found a beautiful monster. That's right, my boy. We found him."

And I knew, however many other finds there would be – and there would be, of course, because I was the girl who saw things other folk didn't – that *this* was a moment I'd remember for the rest of my life.

— ❈ —

"Nearly morning," said Mrs Lark. "Storm's blowing itself out."

"Time for more medicine, do you think?" asked Peggy, but Mrs Lark shook her head.

"Leave it. She seems to have moved beyond the pain now."

The wind rattled the shutters a little but otherwise the room was very still.

"It's so unfair," said Peggy.

"What – dying? Comes to all of us, girl."

"No, not that. It's what the local ladies were talking about in the shop, when I went down there yesterday – Mary Anning should be famous, by rights, they were saying, but those gentlemen scientists took advantage of her and never gave her credit. Did you know she was the one who found all those bones in the rocks and worked out what animals they were? They were from ever so long ago, Mrs Lark – from even longer ago than Adam and Eve. But because she was only a woman and, well, *common*, the scientists and the collectors all acted as if she didn't do *anything*. Those rich old men with their big beards, making it seem they were the only ones. It's just not fair."

"I think she's maybe moved beyond that now, too," murmured Mrs Lark but Peggy didn't reply, for at that moment Mary Anning opened her eyes. They were calm and clear. She reached out her paper-thin hand and put it on Peggy's sleeve.

"Gently does it," Mary whispered. "Nothing to worry about. It's always best after a storm."

She smiled, and for one bright moment, Peggy thought she'd never seen anyone look so happy before.

"It's over," said Mrs Lark. She drew the sheet up to cover Mary Anning's face. Then there was nothing but the shape of her bones to be seen. It was all that remained of the life that was gone.

But, somehow, Peggy could not be sad.

Why I Chose Mary Anning

For many years, I've been crazy about dinosaurs *and* 'the dinosaur woman', Mary Anning. I even dedicated the first of my Victorian detective books to her as an unsung nineteenth-century heroine. It is such a thrill to find even the smallest, most bashed-about fossil from all those millions of years ago, yet Mary Anning discovered complete skeletons of huge ichthyosaurs, plesiosaurs and pterodactyls. At the other end of the size scale, she was also one of the first people to realise that coprolites *aren't* ancient fir cones, but fossilised poo. She received little recognition in her own time, but is now called the Mother of Palaeontology (the study of prehistoric life).

JOAN LENNON

Mary Anning Facts

Mary Anning was born in 1799 and died in 1847. During her lifetime there was a great upsurge of interest in fossils and ideas about dinosaurs and prehistory. Most of the scientists of the day were wealthy men who had the time and the cash to build private collections of whatever they fancied. They bought the fossils that Mary and her family found in the rocks round Lyme Regis – an area now known as the Jurassic Coast. It was not until long after her death that she began to receive the recognition she deserved as a one of the first great finders and identifiers of prehistoric creatures.

The Lad That Stands Before You

*A story about Mary Seacole
(1805–81)*

BY CATHERINE JOHNSON

JUNE 1855, THE CRIMEA

"SIMMS!" CAPTAIN MILLER SHOUTED, so loud I reckoned the Russians in the trench opposite could have heard it. He shouted again but I took no notice. It wasn't my name and I had two pairs of his boots to polish before noon. The sun was out and the guns were quiet. There were even some odd little brown birds, like foreign larks, flying up into the sky and singing.

"Damn and blast!" The captain stared at me. "Who the hell are you?"

"Bayliss, sir," I said. "Private Harry Bayliss."

Captain Miller frowned. "Where's that weasel Simms when I need him?"

"Don't know, sir," I said.

It was a lie. Simms had promised me a bottle of ginger beer from the British Hotel if I did the captain's boots for him. But Simms had been gone hours now. My stomach somersaulted between hope and anger. Hope that Simms was all right and not blasted by the Russians into kingdom come, and anger that he might just be drinking that ginger beer with blue-eyed Sally and forgetting he'd left me, the best friend he'd ever had, to do his chores as well as my own.

A sudden whistle and an ear splitting explosion rocked the trench. Me and the captain ducked. The ground shook and a rain of dust and earth fell down on our heads.

"Damn those Russians!"

The captain stood up slowly, shaking the dust from his cap, and I did the same. I saw him looking at something, staring hard, far away from the shell hole and up towards the battlefield.

"What in heaven's name?" He swore.

I looked where he was looking, and through the smoke I saw a yellow-clad figure, red ribbons flying off a huge straw bonnet, leading a pony – or a mule perhaps. If I hadn't known who she was I would have thought I was dreaming.

"Mrs Seacole." Captain Miller swore again. "The woman is clearly mad! Has she no brain? No fear? Perhaps Negro women like her have neither. We mean to capture the town of Sevastopol in days. She will get herself killed."

I watched as Mother Seacole bent down over the red-coated cavalryman. I wanted to say that me and Simms and every other soldier of the 47th Regiment thought she was lucky. A human charm. Last winter, on the coldest nights, I spent every last penny on her pepperpot stew.

A soldier's life without Mother Seacole's British Hotel, I thought, *would be seven steps closer to hell.*

There was more firing, the French and the Turks returning the Russians' bullets.

Captain Miller yelled for Simms one last time and when no one came, held out a despatch to me.

"You'll have to do," he said. "Take this message to the Redan, to Captain Farrer, and wait for his reply. On the double, boy!"

I looked at him. "The Redan, sir?"

The fort was one of the Russians' most heavily fortified positions outside the city of Sevastopol. We – our soldiers that is – had been here a year. Waiting to attack the Redan. The order would come any day now. We all felt it.

"Idiot boy. I do not expect you to drop my

letter into the czar's lap. This is for Captain Farrer with the advance party." Miller scowled. "Hurry, damn you!"

I ran. Across the ruined land and into the trench that would take me most of the way. Another shell exploded to my left. It knocked me sideways, like a rag doll. I got up, my ears ringing, stumbling like a punch-drunk prize-fighter, my feet slipping and sliding on the dry, sunburnt, battle-scarred earth. One foot in front of the other. Trying not to look at the body flung across my path, arms out as if he'd hug me, colourful shining innards spilling out across his middle like a pedlar's ribbon tray spilt across my path. I had seen so much death I barely slowed.

Until six months ago the only folk I'd seen dead were family. Father, Jeannie, our Tom, and before last Christmas past, Mam. But when they died they were all whole, not blasted apart or shot to pieces.

Before Mam passed over I worked in the mill

with everyone else on our street, but afterwards there seemed no point. I couldn't stand it there any more without Mam – the noise of the looms and the shuttles, the warm damp fug of the weaving room, the air thicker than porridge – so I went to join up. I took our Tom's Sunday coat, which he'd left hanging on the back of the door, and Mother's ring, which I sold for a pair of good boots, then signed my name, joined the 47th Regiment and promised to fight for queen and country. Everyone knew there was a war on. I thought: *Why die here in the damp when I could see the world?*

The recruiting officer believed I was a small fourteen, not a large twelve, and took me on to bang the drum. I banged it from Manchester to London and on through the Middle Sea, past cities that looked as if they had floated in from my dreams – Malta, Venice, Constantinople – till I fetched up here on the Crimean Peninsular. I'd never heard of it in all my life, nor any of the other places with strange names – Sevastopol, Kadikoi and the Black Sea, which isn't black at all. And there were soldiers from all over – *more* places I'd never heard of. Algeria and Sardinia to name just two. Along with us and the French and the Turks, it was like the world all squeezed up into one place.

I had decided I'd rather this than the mill and the churchyard any day of the week.

I ran on past the dead man. Up ahead there was more noise, the repeat of guns, and I crept as close to the edge of the trench as I could. I blinked the dust out of my eyes. And then grinned for exactly three seconds, until I understood exactly what I was seeing.

It was Simms, my best friend, John Simms of the 47th, hurtling round the corner of the trench. Then I froze, because his eyes were wild, his mouth was wide open and in his arms he held a shell – a Russian one, going by the casing. I saw him hurl that thing up and away with every ounce of his might and then I dropped and kissed the earth. Another blast, this time so loud I thought my head had exploded and the sound of a thousand weaving looms and flying shuttles had burst into furious life inside my head.

When I woke up I could not move. I was in a bed with sheets. Real sheets. Perhaps I was dead and this was heaven and I would see Mam again. But there was pain. And I knew from Sunday school was that there would be no pain in heaven. It was my left side, I was sore all along and down to my left leg and my left foot burned as if I had walked barefoot all the way from Manchester to Constantinople. I opened my eyes and was certain this was not heaven, as I found myself in a kind of cupboard made of corrugated iron. My bed was a rough wooden thing shoved up against jars and tins of preserved vegetables and bottles of ginger beer. I smiled. I'd never seen so much food – wait till I told Simms.

I was thinking whether one bottle might not be missed when the door opened and two people came in. A man and a woman.

"Harry Bayliss?" said the man – he had to be a doctor – and by his side, in the same canary yellow dress I'd seen on the battlefield, Mother Seacole.

I tried to sit up.

"There, there," Mother Seacole said and smiled. She was a foot smaller than the doctor, and her brown skin was the selfsame colour as my mam's kitchen table. Her eyes were dark and friendly, and I found myself smiling back at her.

"How is he, Mrs S?" The doctor spoke again.

"Coming along, Doctor."

"Good, good," the doctor said. "Well, Mrs Seacole, it has been good of you to put the patient up, but by the look of him he'll be well enough to come back with me to Miss Nightingale's hospital at Scutari."

Mother Seacole made a face. "We need to keep him a while longer," she said.

"Mother Seacole…" I tried to sit up. "When you found me, was there a Simms there too? John Simms? Was he hurt?" I looked at Mrs Seacole, crossed my fingers and prayed to God he was alive.

"Hush now," Mother Seacole laid one hand upon my forehead. "There's a fever here," she said. "Sally…! Sally! Fetch a cooling poultice and some of my herbal tea." She turned to the doctor. "My patient is not going anywhere till that fever's truly gone."

I thought how jealous Simms would be, the blue-eyed Sally bringing me tea. So long as he wasn't dead. If only he would not be dead.

The doctor leaned close, he smelt of whisky. He looked at Mother Seacole. "Can we see the stump? If there is no suppuration the fever will be of no importance."

I saw Mother Seacole give the doctor a reproving look and for some seconds I had no idea why. Then it trickled into my brain. The word *stump*. The pain in my foot. I sat up and looked down at my legs and let loose a thousand of the choicest, crudest curses known to man, burning the air bluer than a Black Sea summer sky.

"Shh, now." Mother Seacole sat on the bed and put her arms around me. I heard her tell the doctor to come back later when his breath might be sweeter. The doctor reminded her I had no money to pay for my keep and that the hospital in Scutari was the best possible place.

Then he slammed out of the door and I gulped down air until I was sick. I would never see the world now.

Mother Seacole mopped my face with her handkerchief. She rubbed my back as if I were a baby.

"You lost your foot. Cry for it all you like, but it is not coming back."

"I know that," I said, eventually.

"You still have one, more than some folk round here. And you still have a beating heart in your body."

"And no way to make a living, save sitting in the road with a sign around my neck and asking for pennies," I said.

She shrugged. "That is up to you. But you are young. Who knows the future?" She smiled, a quick short smile, and Sally came in with tea. I did not take it straight away.

"The doctor is right." I looked at Sally and Mother Seacole. "I cannot pay," I said. "And I know you run a business here, madam."

"Madam, is it now?" Mother Seacole laughed. "Well, your pockets may be empty, but you cannot go to Scutari neither," she said.

I thought Sally was about to speak but Mother Seacole flashed her a look and they left me to rest, the poultice cool on my forehead.

Only I could not sleep or rest for worry. I sipped my tea and lay on my back listening to the men and horses heading down the road past the British Hotel towards Sevastopol. Where was Simms? How would I live now? I was no use as a soldier nor in the mill.

I finished the tea, feeling suddenly drowsy, my eyes almost closing, when with a start I realised my uniform was hanging over the end of the bed. I looked at myself; I was wearing some kind of nightshirt. Someone had undressed me. I felt sick and more feverish than ever. My heart thump-thumping away in my chest like the horses trotting away to battle. I tried to sit up, but my body felt leaden and I had to fight to keep my eyes open. My best bet was to get away as soon as I could.

That was the last thing I remembered.

I did not know how long I had slept. Mother Seacole was fussing about when I came round.

"There you are," she said.

I remembered my uniform. What did she know?

"You will be all right," she said. "One door shuts and others open."

"They are all shut for me now."

"That is not true," she said. "Look at me! I am an old woman in a ridiculous dress. Upholstered like a chaise in a planter's—" She stopped, checked herself before going on. "Dressed like a holiday beacon in vain hope the Russians will see me and stay their fire while I see to any injured soldiers. I know what it is like to do whatever it takes."

I humphed. "You know nothing about me!"

Mrs Seacole leaned back. "I know this," she said. "I could not let the doctor take you to Scutari."

I flushed and turned away, my cheeks flaming red.

I stared down the bed again. There was a lump

where my right foot steepled the sheet but none where my left foot should have been. I thought of my life in the 47th; I had not only lost my foot but also my friend. The best friend I'd ever had. For surely, even if Simms was still alive, he would not want to know me now. I cried a little but very quietly.

It was two days later that Mother Seacole and Sally had me walking up and down the room with a crutch. My side was still sore, as was my stump, but Mother Seacole said the pain would pass.

The final battle of the siege had begun and the guns boomed for hours on end without stopping. Men, some broken, many worse off than me, passed through heading for the boat to the hospital. Mother Seacole and Sally fed them and helped them and I busied myself unpacking deliveries and winding bandages. I heard them singing marching songs, new songs about this war, and old songs about other wars – 'Over the Hills and Far Away', which was always my favourite, and 'The Lad That Stands Before Ye'.

Sally and me joined in and the sound bounced off the tin roof and made the work go twice as fast. Horses and men poured eastwards towards the city of Sevastopol and there were minutes when I almost forgot the pain in my foot.

I'd just finished rolling up the last of the bandages when Sally came back from the boats and told me she'd found out Simms was alive and well and already laid up in the hospital at Scutari with a shot wound.

At first I felt nothing but joy, overflowing. There were boats to Scutari every day. I could be there in hours. I found my uniform and wriggled into my jacket. I had pulled my cap on when I remembered. I could never go back to the 47th.

That evening, Mother Seacole bustled in wearing red tartan with her red-ribboned bonnet. You would have thought to look at the old bird that it was Christmas.

"Your face is long enough to sweep the floor," she said.

"Simms will think I'm heartless if I never see him again." I looked away.

She shrugged. "You could always write."

I flushed, ashamed. "I can write my name, that is all. He might think I'm just a liar."

"We all lie and that's the truth of it," she said. "I can write for you." She fetched some paper, pen and ink and set them down upon a little table.

"There. Shall we begin? Dear John?"

"Simms," I said. "He is always and only Simms."

"Dear Simms." She made the swooping curling letters unfold upon the paper like a magic trick.

"Truth is, I can't say whether he can read neither."

Mother Seacole put the pen down. "Someone will surely read it to him and he will be pleased to know you are alive and well. He will not want to forget you."

"I cannot tell him everything."

"Perhaps not."

"Then write that he was a good and true friend. And that I will not forget him." I paused.

"Tell him I am alive and well, but now I have no foot I will return to England."

Mother Seacole looked at me. "Sally said you wanted to see the world. Venice, she said."

"How can I do that now?"

"With difficulty." She sighed. "But, I am a firm believer that everything is possible. The British Government did not want me here – did you know that? I wanted to help, I'm as good a nurse as any, but they turned me away so many times."

I shrugged.

"Miss Nightingale did not want me for her hospital in Scutari. Oh no! They saw only one thing about me – the colour of my skin – and they decided they did not like me. But did I listen? Did I let them stop me? No. I came anyway. That is how it is."

"But you have cash, Mother," I said. "Money."

"You think so?" She laughed and she shook like some great brown blancmange. "You do not realise how many fortunes I have made and lost, made and lost again! From Jamaica to Panama to London and to the Black Sea, I have been rich and poor, married and widow." She sighed again. "If you put your mind to it you can make your own life." She looked hard at me. "And I think you have already." She stopped suddenly as Sally put her head round the door.

"Mrs Seacole, you're wanted!"

And Mother Seacole got up and hurried out after Sally.

I looked at the letter, the black curls and squiggles, and hoped to heaven Simms would remember me. I picked up the pen. I had not held one since the day I joined up. Back then I had written *Bayliss, H.*

This time I wrote my true name. *Harriet.*

Why I Chose Mary Seacole

To be honest, I didn't really choose Mary Seacole – she sort of chose me. I'm mixed race, like Mary, and I knew about her already. In fact, my uncle Curtis Johnson made a bust of Mary that was reproduced on one of Jamaica's postage stamps. And one of my big 'things' is people of colour in Britain in the past – we have been here for ever, you know, or at least since Roman times! When I started, I thought I wanted to write about Mary in London, aged about fifteen or sixteen, on her first visit. She never really talked about this trip and there are only two lines in her book about it. It made me think: *A girl from a tiny island in the Caribbean in the biggest city on earth...* But I think that story will have to wait for another time.

One other thing – I've used the word 'Negro' in my story. It's how an officer in the British Army describes Mrs Seacole; the word was in common use and not thought to be derogatory at the time. In her own writing, Mrs Seacole described herself as 'Creole' (meaning 'one born in Jamaica') and sometimes simply as 'brown'.

CATHERINE JOHNSON

Mary Seacole Facts

Mary Seacole was born in Kingston, Jamaica in 1805. She travelled widely as a young woman, visiting London, Panama, Haiti and Cuba. She married in 1836, but six years later her husband died. When the Crimean War broke out in 1854, she responded to Florence Nightingale's call for nurses but was refused. She went to the Crimea under her own steam and set up a hotel. In 1857 she wrote a book about her adventures, *The Wonderful Adventures of Mrs Seacole in Many Lands*, and it was a bestseller. She died in London in 1881 aged 76 and was buried in the cemetery in Kensal Green.

Return to Victoria

A story of Emily Davison (1872–1913)

BY CELIA REES

THE LADY LOOKED NERVOUS. Lizzy smiled at her from the seat opposite, but she didn't smile back. The carriage filled up, everyone excited because they were going to the races, but the lady didn't look at anyone or engage in the general chatter. She stared out of the window or down at her gloved fingers plaiting and unplaiting themselves on her lap.

Lizzy had first noticed her in the booking hall at Victoria Station.

"Single or return?" the man in the ticket office had enquired out of habit. No one asked for a single on Derby Day. Why else would anyone be going to Epsom? The only thing there was the racecourse. Even so, the lady seemed to hesitate. Behind her, the queue grew. Lizzy shifted from foot to foot, the coins for her fare sticky in her hand.

"Single or return?" he squawked again.

"A return," she said at last, as if the idea of it had only just occurred to her. "Of course."

"And what do you want, young lady?" It was Lizzy's turn to be squawked at. His small head shot forward on his thin neck and his sandy hair stuck out like feathers. He looked like a balding Rhode Island Red hen.

"Return to Epsom, please."

Lizzy had been supposed to meet her father at Victoria.

"Under the clock, Libs. Don't be late."

When the great clock clicked past the allotted time, Lizzy bought her own ticket. He'd given her money and instructions.

"If I'm not at there, I'll meet you by the grandstand. Far corner. Left-hand side. You can't miss it."

Lizzy showed her ticket to the man at the barrier and put it in her pocket. Once she'd found a seat on the train, she thought that it would be safer in her purse with her few coppers, a threepence, a sixpence and her mother's little cameo brooch. She opened the small satchel she carried. The purse was next to Angelina, the rag doll her mother had made for her. Aunty Mollie had questioned the inclusion of Angelina.

"Aren't you a bit old for dolls?" she'd asked, as she put a packet of jam sandwiches and a carefully stoppered bottle of cold tea into Lizzy's satchel.

Too old for dolls, but too young to go to the races.

"Are you barmy, Charlie?" Aunt Mollie had said to Lizzy's dad. "She's far too young to go on her own."

"She won't be on her own, *I'll* be with her. She'll love it. Won't you, my poppet?" He'd smiled his famous smile, the one that made people call him a 'real charmer'. "It's the greatest day in the racing calendar."

Except he wasn't, was he?

Aunty Mollie had given him a look that said just that. Lizzy hated it when she was right. *Still*, Lizzy said to herself as she gave Angelina a hug, *I know where to meet him and he'll be there.* He'd absolutely promised.

"Promise, Libs. I swear.' He'd licked his finger and held it up. "Blackswhite and swelpmegawd."

He'd laughed then and she'd laughed back. He'd swept her up into his arms and whirled her around until she was giddy. When he was like that, he really was the best daddy in the world, even if he didn't always keep his promises.

"It's all very well coming here when you feel like it, sweet talking your way around her," Aunty Mollie had said. "You don't have to cope with the tears when you go away again."

Which wasn't fair. Lizzy rarely cried when he left. She saved her tears for later, when everyone was asleep.

"Don't start on at me, Moll!" He'd frowned then, the sulky younger brother. "You know I can't look after her! Since Bonnie went..."

"How many years ago was that, Simon? Six? Seven?"

Her mother had died when Lizzy was four. *Fell Asleep 1907*, it said on her tombstone in Kensal Green Cemetery. Except she hadn't. People who fall asleep wake up. Lizzy's mother died of diphtheria. She never woke up.

"And what have you been doing?" her aunt had gone on. "Going racing. Racketing about on the town with your fancy women. Going to the dogs in more ways than one. If it wasn't for me, she'd be in an orphanage."

Lizzy had felt fear leap, deep down inside her. That's what cousin Rex said when she wouldn't do what he wanted: "You'll end up in the orphanage, you will. And good riddance!"

"Don't you think I don't know that?" Her father twisted the ends of his moustache. "I've tried my best for her. I pay for her keep, don't I? Here!"

He laid notes on the table.

"Did you make these yourself?" Mollie had held one up to the light and pretended to look for signs of forgery before folding the money carefully and tucking it into her apron pocket. "Or did a horse come in?"

"Something like that." He had grinned then. "You know me too well, Sis." He'd given her a peck on the cheek. "Must be off." He'd kissed Lizzy on the top of the head. "Got to see a man about a dog."

That's what he always said. Lizzy had been holding out hopes for a cairn terrier but so far, no dog.

The guard gave a long blast on his whistle. The train moved slowly at first, then faster, the engine giving out great billowing puffs of smoke and steam. Soon the station was behind them. The wide expanse of the Thames glittered in the June sunshine as they crossed over the bridge and then they were moving past sooty buildings, warehouses and factories, the backs of houses, little gardens, tumbledown sheds, outhouses and washing lines. Lizzy sat forward in her seat; she liked the glimpses the train gave of other people's lives.

She was so far forward and so intent on looking out that when the train lurched suddenly, Lizzy nearly ended up in the lady's lap.

"Oh, I'm awfully sorry," she said as she scrambled back into her seat.

"That's quite all right. No harm done." The lady gave the faintest flicker of a smile and carried on staring out of the window.

"I like seeing everything going past," Lizzy said, thinking that the lady must, too, so intent was her gaze.

"Do you?"

"It's interesting, isn't it?"

The lady didn't reply to that. Her eyes were fixed. Her hands worked in her lap. Perhaps she wasn't seeing anything outside at all, just something only she could see inside her own head. Lizzy studied her. She looked very serious. Not cruel, or haughty, or sour; her eyes were kind, but as though she wasn't given very much to smiling, as if there was some sadness in her life.

She certainly stood out from the racegoers. She was well dressed, but in a sober sort of way, in a dark costume and white blouse. More suitable for a funeral than Epsom on Derby Day. Her hat was black straw.

The lady looked back sharply, as if suddenly aware of Lizzy's eyes on her.

"I was just admiring your brooch," Lizzy managed, knowing that it was ill mannered to stare. "I like brooches. I have one that belonged to my mother. It's in my purse because I don't want to lose it. She's dead now."

"Oh, I'm sorry to hear that." The lady glanced down at the pin on her lapel. It looked like a little bunch of violets that had been turned into crystal. "Amethyst, pearl and peridot."

"It's very pretty," Lizzy ventured.

"It's not meant to be just *pretty*." The lady looked severe again. She held the brooch out so that Lizzy could get a clearer look. "It has another meaning. Or at least, the colours do. Green. White. Violet. Initial letters standing for 'Give Women Votes'." She emphasised each word. "Do you know about the suffragettes?"

Lizzy had been with Aunt Mollie on an omnibus delayed by one of the suffragettes' demonstrations. Women dressed in white with green and purple sashes, marching along, chanting, singing, carrying placards.

"Get back to your husbands!" Aunt Mollie had shouted, joining in with the jeering bystanders. "Get back to your children! Get back to your homes!" Then she'd turned to Lizzy. "I don't hold with it," she'd said. "Votes for women? Stuff and nonsense."

Lizzy didn't tell the lady any of that. She just nodded.

"We want the vote so that girls like you will be able to have a say in how this country is run. Without it, wealth and education count for nothing and we will never have equality with men.

When you are old enough, you must join us." The lady was clasping the brooch now. "It is every woman's duty to fight for what should be theirs by right. Remember that."

Lizzy nodded. She could see the sense of it. She looked round at the men in the compartment. Why should they be allowed to vote when the ladies couldn't? It did not seem fair. And what about Rex, her odious cousin? When they both grew up, he'd be able to vote and she wouldn't, even though she was miles cleverer and kinder and nicer, as were her girl cousins, for that matter. No, that was all wrong.

"Are you travelling alone?" the lady asked.

"Yes. I'm meeting my daddy at the race course."

"It's an awfully big place." The lady looked doubtful. "With very many people."

"He's told me where to meet him. My name's Lizzy, by the way," she added, to stop her asking any more questions. "Lizzy's short for Elizabeth."

"How do you do, Elizabeth." The lady held out her gloved hand. "I'm Emily. Emily Wilding Davison."

"Are you meeting someone?" Lizzy enquired, thinking she ought to carry on the conversation now that they had been properly introduced.

"No. I'm alone," Miss Davison said, as though it was important. "I do have an appointment…" She consulted a little pocket watch. "But not for a while yet."

"Next stop, Epsom," a voice called along the corridor. "Epsom, next stop."

There was a bustle in the carriage, with people getting things down from the luggage nets.

When the train stopped at the station, the door swung open but Lizzy hesitated. The platform was a sea of hats – top hats, bowlers, caps and boaters, wheels of tulle, feathers and flowers. She had never seen so many people. There didn't seem room to move between them.

Miss Davison held out her gloved hand. "Come with me."

"Which way is it?" Lizzy asked.

"We'll just follow the crowd."

The road to the racecourse was white with dust and choked with traffic. Omnibuses, charabancs, motorcars, horse-drawn carts and carriages crawled in a long line, while pedestrians surged along beside the vehicles. Lizzy was glad she had a hand to hold, or she might never have gone anywhere at all

The crowds thickened near the entrance, then spilled through the gates onto the racecourse proper. It was very much bigger than Lizzy had supposed and there were even more people milling about everywhere.

"Where have you arranged to meet your father?" Miss Davison asked. She still held Lizzy's hand.

"Up at the grandstand. On the left-hand side."

"Let's go there, shall we?"

There were all sorts of people here, from lords in top hats arm in arm with ladies in white dresses to chaps in flat caps and check jackets. Gypsies carried trays of charms and urchins darted about through the crowd. Lizzy held on to Miss Davison with one hand and her satchel with the other.

They fought their way past funfairs and sideshows and tents selling refreshments, where men stood, holding pints of beer and glasses of whisky. Lizzy's father wasn't with them and he wasn't queuing at any of the bookies' stands, so he was probably waiting for her at the corner of the grandstand, as he said he would be.

"Is this the place?" Miss Davison asked.

"I think so," Lizzy looked about but there was no sign of her father.

The crowd had ceased its milling and had thickened, spreading out, snaking along the rails. Some were waving their hats and cheering. Lizzy could hear hooves thundering and the jockeys' bright colours went flashing past, yellow and purple, blue and red, and the heads of the horses, chestnut, jet, amber and white.

"Is that the race? Has it started?"

"No." Miss Davison shook her head. "They are just cantering up to the start. But I must leave you now." She seemed agitated. "I really must go."

"That's all right." Lizzy smiled up at her. "Daddy will be here soon. Bound to be."

"Have you got everything you need?" Miss Davison asked. "Money? Your ticket?"

In case he doesn't come, Lizzy thought, knowing Miss Davison was too nice to say so.

"Oh, yes. I—"

She put her hand down to her satchel. The straps were open, when she was sure that she'd done them up. She looked inside, curious as to how that could have happened. Angelina was still there, and her sandwiches and the bottle of tea, but her purse was gone. She squeezed her eyes shut then looked again. Still the same thing. She sorted through with shaking fingers.

"Oh, no!" She felt tears starting.

"What on earth's the matter?"

"My purse! It's gone!" Lizzy's voice was wobbling. "My ticket, money, everything." She put her hand to her mouth. "Mummy's brooch!"

"Don't cry." Miss Davison knelt down awkwardly. She offered a handkerchief to stem the tears, then opened her small handbag. "Here's some money," she held out some coins, "and have my ticket."

Lizzy looked down at the little beige stub. Epsom Race Course to Victoria.

"But how will you get back?"

"Don't you worry about that." Miss Davison stood up. "Here." She unpinned the brooch from her lapel. "Have this, too. And remember what it stands for."

"Give Women Votes."

"Good girl." She gave her first smile and ruffled Lizzy's curls. "Never forget that."

"I won't."

Lizzy tucked the brooch in her pocket with the handkerchief and the coins – only to find the stub of her *own* ticket. It must have been there all along. How silly! But it was too late. Miss Davison was now shouldering her way through the crowd as if she was in a tearing hurry.

"There you are," a voice said. "I've been looking everywhere!"

Lizzy hardly heard him. She was already dodging through the crowd, shouting, "Miss Davison! I say, Miss Davison!"

Lizzy caught up with her just before the rails.

"Here," she gasped out, thrusting the stub into the lady's hand.

"What's this?" Miss Davison looked down as if she'd never seen such a thing before.

"It's your ticket."

She took it with a muttered "Thank you," and pushed her way on through the crowd.

Lizzy was yanked backwards.

"What the devil do you think you're doing?" her father shouted down at her. "Dickens of a job to find you, then you go haring off! Still, Tattenham Corner. Not a bad spot to watch the race. Not a bad spot at all… They're under starter's orders." He heaved her up on to his shoulders. "Up you go!"

Lizzy could now see over the heads of the crowd. There was a great cheer as the race started. People leaned forward, craning their necks for a first glimpse as the drumming of hooves turned to thunder and the horses came down the hill to the corner. They were going at the most tremendous gallop, ears back, nostrils flaring, their jockeys riding high, out of their saddles. The leaders were bunched together, iron to iron. The crowd were yelling, screaming out names as the horses streamed by – *Craganour, Aboyeur, Nimbus, Day Comet, come on!*

"Who's in the lead?" her father called up to her.

They were flashing past now. Lizzy had no idea that horses could run so fast.

"Colours!" he shouted. "What colours?"

"Yellow and purple just in front of black and white."

"Good. Good!"

Her father was jigging up and down with excitement. Lizzy felt like a jockey herself.

The leaders had passed now, the followers strung out behind them. There was a gap between one horse and another. Suddenly, a figure ducked under the rails and into the thundering charge of horses. A woman. In a dark dress and hat. It was her.

She stepped straight out. One horse missed her, but the next caught her full force. Her hat bowled over and over as she was flung aside like a bundle of washing. The horse baulked and stumbled, pitching the jockey clear over its head.

The rest of the field galloped on, swerving to avoid the two bodies lying in their path, one curled in a ball, the other sprawled and still.

For a moment, there was silence, then someone shouted, "The king's horse! It's the king's horse!"

People were running across the course now, crowding round the figures on the ground, but the race went on.

"What's happened?" Lizzy's father called up to her.

"Someone stepped out..." Lizzy started. "She's... I think she's..."

She couldn't speak. Her throat had closed up with sorrow for the lady who had been so kind and now lay broken.

"Thank God she didn't ruin the race. I'm going to the finish. See who's won." He set her down. "I've got ten pounds on Aboyeur." He ran off across the field. "Come on!"

"No, I'm staying here."

"Please yourself. Meet me..." But his voice was lost in the roaring cheers that marked the end of the race.

Lizzy turned away. What did she care who'd lost or who'd won?

The crowd began to mutter. There was disagreement about the winner. People were walking away now, wanting to find out what had happened at the finish, moving off from the figure on the ground.

Lizzy went to the rails. Miss Davison was beyond anyone's help but Lizzy didn't want to leave her. She'd keep watch until they took her away. She heard someone say that Aboyeur had won. Her father's horse, at 100-1. She knew she wouldn't see him again today. But what did it matter? She had a return ticket in her pocket. Lizzy reached in to make sure and touched the brooch Miss Wilding had given her. She could make her own way now.

Why I Chose Emily Davison

It is over a hundred years since Emily Wilding Davison died under the king's horse during the 1913 Epsom Derby. The whole dramatic incident was caught by early newsreel cameras. Did she mean to kill herself, or was it an accident? The debate goes on to this day, revolving around her purchase of a return ticket and new techniques for analysing the film footage. Whatever her motives, her action had an enormous impact.

I've always been profoundly moved by the story of Emily Davison, who was willing to lay down her life for her cause. Anyone who has been close to horses at full gallop can have little doubt that she meant to die that day. The suffragettes showed that they were equal to men in courage, passion, hope and endurance and, eventually, Emily's sacrifice and that of many others would result in women being allowed to vote on an equal footing with men.

It was a right hard won. It is our duty to use it.

CELIA REES

Emily Davison Facts

Emily Wilding Davison was born in Blackheath, London, in 1872. She was hardworking and intelligent and in 1895, spent a term at Oxford University. Although Oxford did not award degrees to women at the time, she achieved First Class Honours in English. Emily was finally given her degree by London University and became a teacher.

In 1897, the National Union of Women's Suffrage Societies was founded in the United Kingdom, to fight for women's right to vote. New Zealand had been the first country to grant this right to women, four years earlier, in 1893, and South Australia had followed shortly afterwards, in 1894.

The more radical and militant Women's Social and Political Union was established in 1903 by Emmeline Pankhurst. It adopted the colours purple, white and green to symbolise dignity, purity and hope. Their motto was 'Deeds Not Words'. Emily Davison joined the WSPU in 1906 and left teaching two years later to dedicate herself to violent campaigning. Between 1909 and 1912, she was imprisoned several times, for militant acts such as obstruction and stone throwing, for breaking windows in the House of Commons and for setting fire to postboxes. Going on hunger strike while in prison was common among suffragettes and many suffered force-feeding as a result, including Emily.

In 1913, Emily Davison was killed after stepping in front of the king's horse at the Epsom Derby.

It wasn't until 1918 that the Representation of the People Act was passed, giving women over the age of 30 who owned property the right to vote. Ten years later, the act was extended to give the vote to all women over the age of 21. Finally, fifteen years after the death of Emily Wilding Davison, women had achieved the same voting rights as men.

The Colours of the Day

A story about Amy Johnson
(1903–41)

BY ANNE ROONEY

"COME HERE, LITTLE GIRL."

Ruby bristled.

"I'm not a little girl," she said. "I'm Ruby Aurora—"

"All right!" The woman held up a fatly gloved hand. "I don't need to know who you are. I just have to transport you. Now, let's get you in the plane – Ruby."

Ruby had never been in a plane, but tried to look as if she did it every day and wasn't at all excited. She straightened her woollen hat and matching coat, picked up her smart little suitcase and started across the rigid, frosted grass. The woman took long strides. It was impossible for Ruby to walk elegantly, as a film star would – she had to skip and run to keep up.

"Slow down!" Ruby shouted, cross at this woman who was spoiling it all. She wished there was someone to wave her off, but there wasn't. Her mother was in hospital with appendicitis and her father was sitting in the War Cabinet in London. Mummy's chauffeur, who had brought her to the airport, had gone. No one was watching – not even the engineers, who were busy with other planes.

"I'm Amy," the woman said. "Have you flown before?"

Ruby shook her head. She didn't actually want to say no, but she couldn't lie.

"Then it will be exciting."

Amy helped Ruby on to the wing and in through a little door – an upside-down triangle, opening into the body of the plane.

"Go to the right and wait," she said. "Sit there and be quiet. You can come to the cockpit when I tell you to."

There were no seats. Ruby crouched uncomfortably and listened as Amy clattered around in the front of the plane. Someone else climbed in and started talking. It made Ruby cross – she was being treated like a bit of baggage. She sighed loudly and rattled some of the bits of metal stuff that lay about, hoping that Amy would hear her.

A man's voice was talking about weather, telling Amy not to go, but she laughed. Then the engines started and Ruby couldn't hear any more chat. The smell of cigarette smoke drifted back to Ruby. It made her even more cross – they were just sitting smoking, ignoring her!

But soon, the door slammed shut, and Amy called her to the cockpit.

"Sit there."

Ruby wriggled into the seat beside Amy, the leather squeaking against the backs of her legs. She fixed her face into a stern, bored look.

"Are you excited?" Amy asked.

Ruby nodded.

"Then look excited!" Amy said. "Let's get going. And don't just shake or nod your head when I ask you a question. I can't spend my time looking at you, I have to look at the instruments."

There were a lot of instruments: banks of dials and switches and levers.

The plane bumped over the frozen grass, gathering speed. Then the bumping stopped and Ruby's stomach lurched as they lifted into the air. The ground dwindled away beneath her and she squealed; the excitement wouldn't stay inside any longer. After all – why waste something so good by trying to look grown-up? Perhaps her mother was wrong to worry so much what other people thought. It was a relief to let her excitement out, like taking off some garment that was too tight – one that had been comfortable once, but was now outgrown.

"It's all getting so small! This must be what a bird sees!" she shouted over the noise. Amy glanced at her, and smiled for the first time. A few flakes of snow splattered themselves against the windshield, then a few more.

"It's snowing!" Ruby called. "Is that safe? I mean, in the plane?"

"Perfectly," Amy said. "We'll be above the snow soon."

"How can we be?"

Ruby soon found out. It was like stepping outside on a foggy day. Everything vanished into a swaddling of mist. Water spotted the windows, then froze into jagged lines. The lines reminded Ruby of bare branches standing out against the sky.

"We're inside the clouds now," Amy said as

the plane bumped and bounced. "It's lumpy to fly through. Do you feel sick?"

"I'm never sick," Ruby said. "I have an iron constitution. My nanny always said so."

Amy's jaw tightened. Then she pulled the funny, W-shaped control wheel hard to the left and the plane tipped sideways.

Ruby did feel a little bit sick after all. But she wasn't going to say so. She gripped the sides of her seat and stared ahead into the nothingness.

At last, they came out of the cloud into dazzling, clear, blue sky. But in just a little while, the plane churned and tossed and bucked up and down like a naughty horse, all over again.

"Is it dangerous?" Ruby asked, feeling even more sick.

"It could be. Are you scared?"

"Of course not," Ruby said, lifting her chin.

"Well, perhaps you should be. We're a long way up. We can't see the ground. There are barrage balloons and wires and all kinds of things between here and Oxford. And hills."

Ruby shifted in her seat. "Are you trying to make me scared?" she said.

Amy laughed. "Maybe a little. It's good to be cautious. If you're not careful of dangers, you can come to a sticky end."

"Have you ever crashed?" Ruby asked.

"Yes."

Amy fiddled with some instruments and Ruby waited for her to carry on. She didn't.

"When did you crash?" Ruby asked eventually.

"In India. I was flying all the way from England to Australia and crashed on the way. But then I crashed again when I got to Australia, and that was how I met my husband, Jim! Did you know that?"

Ruby shook her head, then remembered what Amy had said about speaking.

"No," she said. "I didn't know. Did you go all the way to Australia in one go?"

"No. A plane can't go that far without stopping for more fuel."

"Will you tell me about the crash? Were you dreadfully hurt?"

"I wasn't. They were little crashes, and only Jason was hurt."

"Jason?"

"My plane."

Ruby laughed. "Your plane had a name?"

"Yes. Don't you name your dolls?"

"I'm too big for dolls. Could you mend Jason?"

"Yes. And I flew on, all the way to Australia. But three years later I flew from London to New York with my husband. We crashed again, and then we were both hurt."

"Don't you die if you crash?" Ruby asked.

"Not always, or I wouldn't be here, would I?" Amy said.

Ruby picked at her dress and didn't answer. But being cross was boring.

"I hope we don't crash today," she said, after a while.

"So do I."

"Might we?"

"No."

They flew in silence for a long while. Every now

and then, Amy tapped an instrument.

"Dratted thing," she grumbled.

"What is it?" Ruby asked.

"The compass. I don't think it works. And through this cloud, I can't see where we are."

"Are we going to crash?"

"No," Amy said.

The plane dipped down, back into the clouds, and ice crazed the windshield again. As they emerged, the snow started building up, until neither of them could see out.

"Daddy's car has wipers to wipe the snow away," Ruby said. "Why doesn't the plane have wipers?"

"It just doesn't," Amy said, her voice snappish. "Can you see anything at all down there? It's blinding."

The snow slid from the windshield as the plane turned slightly. Ruby peered downwards. White flakes fell beneath them, around them, in front of them. She could see nothing but falling white.

Amy tapped the compass again and sighed. "We should have got to Kidlington ages ago," she said. "We'll have to head east, towards London. There are landmarks to spot."

"But I can't go to London! London is where the bombs are," Ruby said. "That's why Mummy and I had to go away. Daddy doesn't want me to be in London because of the bombs. He wants me to stay with my auntie in the countryside where it's safe."

"Yes, I'm sure he does. But I don't suppose one night will hurt," Amy said. "And it's not as though we've got a lot of options just now."

"But my daddy said. And he's in the War Cabinet and—" Ruby stopped. "Daddies don't always know the right thing to do, do they?"

Amy laughed.

"No, they don't. My daddy doesn't like me flying. Though he's happier now I'm flying around Britain than when I was flying to Australia, or America, or Moscow. This is much safer."

Ruby wriggled down into her seat, comforted to hear that they were safer than they would be flying to Moscow, wherever that was.

"It's a bit cold up here," she said at last.

Amy didn't answer.

They flew on, through the whiteness. It was tiring to look at, so Ruby looked around the inside of the plane.

"There are lots of dials and things. How do you know what they all do?"

Amy replied to all her questions, but the answers were quite hard to understand. Eventually, Ruby stopped asking and they sat in silence until the plane had climbed above the clouds again.

"It's like being dead," Ruby said at last.

"What do you mean?"

"Above the clouds is where heaven is, isn't it? I hope being dead isn't so noisy and cold, though."

"Yes, being above the clouds is heaven," Amy said.

She smiled, and Ruby thought she looked much nicer when she was smiling.

The blue sky faded to grey, the darkness coming in from above, it seemed, for when Ruby looked upwards it was dark there already.

"My daddy is in the War Cabinet," Ruby said again. "But I don't think he really knows as much as he says. He sent me and Mummy away because of the bombs, but there are bombs in Liverpool, too."

"There are bombs everywhere, I'm afraid. That's the thing with wars. But he obviously cares a lot for you. It must have taken a bit of work to get you this flight," Amy said.

The dark shapes of barrage balloons loomed out of the distance, vast, concentrated bubbles of grey in the gloom.

"We must be near London," Amy said. "The balloons are above the clouds because they're expecting an attack."

"Will we be in a dogfight?" Ruby asked. "Do we have any guns?"

"No. We don't have any guns. If we're in a fight, we just lose."

Ruby glanced across to see if Amy was joking. "But can't we fight at all?"

"We won't need to," Amy said. "It's not going to happen – don't worry so much."

They flew on, keeping the balloons on their left.

"We're going to dip below the clouds again," Amy said. "I need to get a bearing from something. Do you have sharp eyes?"

"Very," Ruby said. "Nanny says—"

"Good. You keep a look-out for the wires that tether the balloons. We don't want to get caught up in them."

The cloud crusted the windshield with ice again, making a jaggedy pattern just as it did inside the windows of the cold house in Liverpool.

That didn't happen in the nice house in London where they usually lived, Ruby thought. She wished they hadn't had to leave. But then she remembered how Daddy had said everyone has to make sacrifices in a war.

As they descended, a shaft of light stabbed into the cloud and passed away to their right.

"Drat it!" Amy snapped. "Searchlights."

Soon, a church spire pricked through a thin mist far below and the crawling shapes of buildings broke through in patches. Then without warning the darkness was sliced into triangles by more beams of light swishing across the sky.

Ack-ack-ack-ack.

A sound like the battering of hail, but a hundred times louder, rocked the plane.

Ack-ack-ack-ack.

"What's happening?" Ruby squealed.

Ack-ack-ack-ack.

"Are they firing at us?" Ruby asked, panic now bursting out of her so violently she started to shake. "Radio them we're English!"

"We don't have a radio. The plane's only just been built – the radio hasn't been fitted yet."

"Why did Daddy send me in a dangerous plane?" Ruby whimpered.

"Your father just sent the order for you to be transported. He doesn't choose the plane. And you're lucky to get any plane. There are more important things to think about in this war than ferrying little girls around!"

"That's not fair!" Ruby said, her voice trembling.

"Sorry," Amy said, and patted Ruby's knee.

Amy riffled through a rack of canisters behind her seat and fitted one into a pistol.

"Are we going to shoot them?" Ruby asked. "I thought you said we didn't have any guns?"

"No," Amy said. "It's not a gun for shooting bullets. It can't hurt anyone."

Amy put the pistol into a chute behind the seat and pulled the trigger. Ruby heard a bang and felt a rush of cold air. Then something streamed across the sky with a whooshing sound and yellow smoke drifted away beneath them.

"What's that smoke?" Ruby screamed. "Have we been hit?"

"No. It's a flare. They're a bit like fireworks – they pour coloured smoke into the air. We use a different coloured smoke on different days. They show we're friendly – it's a kind of secret code."

Amy sent off a second flare, trailing crimson smoke that bled into the falling snow.

"We're friends?" Ruby calmed a little, glowing at the thought of counting a famous aviator as her friend.

"No, I mean we're a friendly plane – British, not German." Amy looked at her. Then she added, "But we can be friends, too."

Ack-ack-ack-ack.

Amy wrenched the wheel to the right as the beam of a searchlight slashed across their plane, stalled, returned and locked on to them. She reached behind the seat again and a second pair of flares streamed beneath them.

Ack-ack-ack-ack.

"Blast them! We're not an enemy plane!" Amy said. "They can see that from today's colours!"

She swung the plane into the searchlight beam. "We can't dodge them. Look, Ruby, we've got to do something brave. Are you brave?"

Ruby nodded, but she didn't feel very brave. Then she remembered and said, "Yes," rather quietly.

"Good girl." Amy patted Ruby's knee again. "Let's show ourselves to the chaps manning the anti-aircraft guns. Show them we have no black crosses, no guns – we're not a German bomber."

"Not enemies," Ruby added.

"No, not enemies at all. Just Amy Johnson, aviator heroine, coming home. With her friend Ruby!"

Now all the lights locked on to them. The beams shone up around the cockpit, picking out the swirling snowflakes in their unearthly dance in the currents around the plane. Amy's face glowed in the light.

But the next bullets came straight through the cockpit.

Ruby clung to Amy's neck, too terrified to wail or even speak.

Ack-ack-ack-ack. Ack-ack-ack-ack.

Then the fire started. Flames leaped up at the tip of a wing and began to nibble their way along the fabric.

"We have to bail!" Amy shouted through Ruby's stranglehold. "Come on, let go of me. You have to be brave, remember."

She uncurled Ruby's fingers from the collar of her flying jacket and moved the girl gently back into her seat. Ruby froze, letting Amy do it.

"Are you hurt?" Amy shouted above the roar of engines and rushing wind.

Ruby turned big, scared eyes towards her and shook her head.

"Good. You'll have to jump."

Ack-ack-ack-ack.

"But I don't have a parachute!" Ruby cried.

"I do. I'll hold you. Come on." But all the certainty had gone from Amy's voice.

She pulled on Ruby's arm, and motioned to her to climb out of her seat. They clambered into the back of the plane, where Ruby had crouched earlier, before they took off.

Ruby watched Amy struggle with her parachute pack, tightening and testing straps, her fingers trembling. Their plane dropped lower, spluttering and tipping towards its hurt wing. As a search beam swung below them, it flashed over rippled darkness and the end of a ship.

"Look! Water!" Ruby shouted, peering downwards.

"Damn it!" Amy shouted. "Where on earth are we?"

"But water is good," Ruby said. "It can't hurt if we dive right."

Amy said nothing. When Ruby looked across, she saw Amy was shaking.

"I – I don't like parachutes," Amy said, with a nervous laugh. "Always dreaded having to bail out. I just don't like heights. How silly is that for a pilot?"

Ruby put her hand on the sleeve of Amy's thick leather jacket. "How does it open?" she asked.

Amy, her hand trembling, guided Ruby's fingers to the ripcord. "We have to pull this. Then it opens."

"Nanny says it's always best to get bad things over and done with quickly," Ruby said. "How do we get out?"

Amy pointed at the door they'd come in through, but didn't make a move to open it.

Ack-ack-ack-ack.

The plane tilted hard to the left and they both stumbled.

Flames crawled from the tail, too, now. Their orange light flickered over diagrams stencilled on the door. Ruby traced them with a finger, followed the instructions and let a blast of freezing wind rip into the plane.

Instantly, Amy clutched her from behind,

gripping her so tightly round the waist the breath was squeezed out of her.

"Hold on!" Amy yelled. "The wind can whisk you away!"

Ruby could feel Amy's body shaking, even through her thick leather aviator coat.

"Can you swim? I can swim really well," Ruby yelled back. She twisted round to look at Amy, but the woman didn't answer. "It'll be just like a dive at the swimming pool," Ruby went on, turning back to face the tugging wind. "Only, a little further. Shall I count to three? And then we jump? Don't look down. One…"

Ack-ack-ack-ack.

"Two…"

Ack-ack-ack-ack.

The engine noise died and a sheet of flame spread along the wing towards the door.

"They've hit the fuel line!" Amy shouted.

"Thank you, Miss Johnson, for a lovely flight," Ruby shouted. "Three!"

Ruby leaned forward with all her own weight, imagining she was on the diving board at the lido.

It only takes a second, she thought, and then it will be all right.

Then Amy jumped – or Ruby pulled her; Ruby couldn't tell. They fell together into a wall of freezing wind. Ruby's fingers found the cord and pulled. She watched the parachute unfurl, snaking into a long, floppy line above them, then exploding into its canopy, jolting them almost to a standstill. The cold was extreme, like needles driven into her body all over.

Ruby clung to Amy's arms, crossed over her chest, and counted as they swung down through the snow. Four, five, six...

Lumps of burning plane hurtled past in a blur of orange light, streaming flames.

Seven, eight...

The pieces splashed into the water, hissed and vanished.

Nine...

Silence. Its suddenness made Ruby's ears ring.

Ten, eleven.

And a light flashed across them.

Ack-ack-ack-ack.

— ✳ —

Their impact with the water tore Ruby from Amy's arms. The girl plunged deep into the icy Thames.

When Amy surfaced, gulping in air and water, every part of her hurt.

"Please, somebody help!" she called into the darkness, and at last, a light shone in her face.

Ruby's body floated beside her, tendrils of crimson weaving into the river water, the little girl's mouth open in a small, silent 'oh' of surprise.

Behind Amy, the last glimmer of sunset faded over the estuary, and crimson and ruby leaked into black.

Why I Chose Amy Johnson

Suspended from the ceiling of the Science Museum in London is a tiny, dull green De Havilland Gypsy Moth biplane with the name Jason stencilled near the cockpit. In 1930, in this fragile-looking machine, little bigger than a car, Amy Johnson became the first woman to make a solo flight from England to Australia. The trip of 10,000 miles took twenty days, with frequent stops to refuel – the plane could fly for only thirteen hours at a time. The bravery (or stupidity) embodied in such a journey, taken in such a plane, is awe-inspiring.

Amy was a hard-nosed, tough woman – she had to be in order to be taken seriously as a female pilot in the early days of flying, a world dominated by men. She was brave, resilient, confident and passionate about flying. She did not have any children of her own, and would have found dealing at close quarters with a child like Ruby quite a challenge!

ANNE ROONEY

Amy Johnson Facts

Amy Johnson was born in Hull, in the north of England, in 1903. She went to university (in Sheffield), which was unusual for a woman at that time, and later became the first qualified female ground engineer for planes. She first flew in 1928 and she became the first woman to fly solo from Britain to Australia two years later when she was just twenty-six years old. She went on to make other historic flights, including non-stop from London to Moscow and from England to South Africa.

In the Second World War, Amy joined the Air Transport Auxiliary (ATA) and worked delivering new and repaired planes around Britain. It was on one of these flights that the Airspeed Oxford plane she was flying crashed into the Thames estuary near Iwade on 5th January 1941. She had gone off course on a flight from Blackpool, near Liverpool, to Kidlington, near Oxford. Details of Amy's final flight and its purpose are in classified war documents which are still secret. Amy was alive on impact but died in the Thames; her body was not recovered. Captain Fletcher of the HMS Haslemere, which was in the Thames at the time, died trying to rescue Amy. People at the scene insisted that there were two bodies from the plane in the water, but the second person was never recovered or identified.

In 1999, Tom Mitchell claimed to have been one of the men who shot Amy Johnson down, believing her plane to be an enemy craft when she gave the wrong colour signal. He said they had been told never to reveal their role in her death. The account is disputed.

Please Can I Have a Life?

A story about the Greenham Common Women (1981–2000)

BY LESLIE WILSON

1986

I've done it. I'm here.

I'm standing in a crowd of Peace Women, waiting for a convoy of nuclear missiles to arrive back at their base. Only maybe I won't see anything, because there's a line of police in front of me, facing me. Their faces are blank, like machines.

It's two in the morning and it's bitter cold. I keep stamping my feet to try and get the feeling back into them.

I can hear the convoy engines roaring now and the women around me start shouting.

"BLOOD ON YOUR HANDS!"

The cruise missiles have been out on exercise at Salisbury Plain; now they're coming back to the base, and suddenly I'm so scared of seeing them. Because then I'll have to believe it's true.

Every missile in that convoy that's coming is ten times as powerful as the bomb that flattened the whole city of Hiroshima. There are four missiles in every launcher, and I know there are four launchers, so that's a hundred and sixty times worse than Hiroshima. Margaret Thatcher and the American President want to use them to fight a nuclear war in Europe. They'll hide in bomb-proof bunkers when the Russians bomb us back, but the rest of us have been handed a leaflet that tells us to build a hide-out under the stairs with a couple of mattresses for protection.

I'm shivering, not just with the cold.

I stand on tiptoe and now I can see between a couple of police helmets. There it is, the first missile launcher; it's big and ugly with huge, pulverising tyres – and someone's thrown paint on it.

It's really true! A silly childish bit of me kept hoping there weren't any nuclear weapons, not really. But that thing is all my worst nightmares… I couldn't possibly look at it and pretend.

"BLOOD ON YOUR HANDS!" I scream, so loud it makes my throat sore, and, "YOU'RE CRAZY! WICKED!"

I'm crying and I don't care.

A woman tries to break through the police line, but they push her off and give her a couple of kicks. She's staggering, she's hurt.

"PIGS!" I shout.

The policeman in front stares at me. He says, "There's nothing I wouldn't mind doing to one of you lot."

The convoy's gone inside the base, and I'm sitting in the open beside a smoking wood fire, getting my hands warm, drinking hot tea that tastes weird because it's got soya milk in it. There don't seem to be a lot of women there. I thought there'd be hundreds camping out.

The woman who gave me the tea asks me what my name is.

"I'm Blue," I say.

She's old enough to be my mum, and she looks at me like a teacher. Okay, like a kind teacher – but I wish she wouldn't.

"I'm Jane. You look very young, Blue."

Oh, no.

"Does it matter how old I am?"

"It's really tough here. Believe me. When the council comes and evicts us, that's bad, and vigilantes come…"

How old should I say I am? "I'm sixteen," I say.

They're not going to send me away, are they? I can't go home!

She doesn't look convinced, but she asks me if I've got a survival bag, and when I say no, she gets one for me. It belongs to a woman who's gone away for a week. They'll get me my own one later, she says, from a place in Newbury where they keep spares. They can't keep them here because of the evictions. I've got warm clothes though, and food. It's not all bad that Dad's made me into a slave and I have to do the shopping.

I'm in a tent with another woman. She's asleep, I'm not. I'm too wound up. A woman's sitting outside by the fire, keeping watch. There's a collie dog, too, a girl dog (of course), but she's not friendly. I hope she'd bark, though, if anyone came.

Jane said sometimes drunks come and pee into the tents. That's disgusting. I went to pee in the bushes; that was embarrassing, and the women made jokes about peeing on a Mod Plod, that's Ministry of Defence police. Now I think about the police kicking that woman and saying there's nothing they'd mind doing to one of us. Why? Why is it so awful not to want nuclear war?

Mum was against the cruise missiles. One of the last things she wrote was a letter to our MP about them. *No,* I tell myself. *Don't think about her.*

I creep out of the tent to sit with the woman who's on watch. I take my Gore-Tex jacket to sit in, because it's really cold.

"How long have you been here?" I ask.

"A year.' She's not that much older than me, sixteen or seventeen, maybe? She's short and solid and she's got a lovely friendly grin. She's called Kate.

I stare into the fire, seeing the white-hot wood falling apart. If a nuclear bomb falls, it'll vaporise the place it lands – Ground Zero – but further out there'll be a zone where everything just bursts into flames, and nobody will be able to put them out. Partly because they'll be on fire too. The mattress-shelters won't help anyone. The lucky people still further out get to die of radiation sickness.

She makes us more tea in a kettle that's covered

in thick tarry stuff from the fire.

"What do you do here, at the peace camp?"

"Well, partly we're just here so people can't ignore what's behind that fence. But some of us break into the base. Spray-paint. Get arrested. Go to court and argue that preparing for nuclear war is a crime."

That sounds scary. "How do you do that?"

"The law says it's okay to commit a crime, if it's to stop a greater crime happening. Anyway, you don't have to get arrested unless you want to. Then, when they take the convoy down to Salisbury Plain, we track it."

"What exactly do they do there?"

"They practise for nuclear war, when they'd disperse into the countryside. And they do survival exercises – but they're not as good at that as we are." She grins. "They have lovely portaloos down there to *survive* with."

I say, "It's all insane, isn't it?"

"Strategically," she goes on, "our cruise missiles fly so low, they could hit Moscow and the Russian early warning system wouldn't spot them.

So NATO could launch a strike on Russia and hope to win. But it'd be a gamble. Chances are, the Russians would launch a counter-attack and we'd be cooked. You're right, it *is* insane. It's all those men in charge, they think violence is the only thing that works. And Mrs Thatcher – but she's just like a man anyway."

I say, "And people just carry on with their lives, as if nothing was wrong! Like my friend's mum, getting excited about her new en-suite shower room – what does that matter when maybe the whole world's going to be wiped out?"

Kate grins. "Yeah, but showers are a great thing when you live out here. We're allowed to go to the Quaker meeting house in Newbury and use their shower room, it's bliss."

"I've been so scared," I say to Kate. Suddenly, I'm crying again. "I mean, all the time, day and night. It won't leave me alone."

She puts her arm round me. "I know. But listen, it feels better when you're doing something about it."

Kate tells me what to do if there's an eviction. I have to grab my stuff and hold it, or put it into the van. Someone designed the tents so you can pick them up and hold them over your arm. Then the bailiffs, who do the evictions, can't touch them. It sounds scary, but cool.

I sit up with her till morning, when she makes porridge for us both on the fire.

"You need a lot of hot things out here."

She's right. It's lovely to feel the porridge going down.

Then I go to sleep and don't wake up till four in the afternoon. There's a Mum-age woman from Reading who's brought a pot of vegan soup and some vegan chocolate cake. When she sees me, she gives me that 'why aren't you at school' look.

Like my year tutor, last autumn.

"You're having a lot of days off ill. Is everything all right at home? How's your mother?"

"She's okay," I mumbled.

She wasn't. She had really bad MS and she

couldn't speak any longer and nobody except me could guess what she wanted. I'd been looking after her all summer and how could I just go back to school and leave her? So I truanted and forged sick notes. I'm so glad I did. Dad didn't care enough to stop working and help Mum. And one day she just died, suddenly, lying on the bed. Her heart gave out, the doctor said.

I hope the woman with the soup – she's called Lindsey – won't ask me how old I am. What's the point of school anyway, if there's going to be a nuclear war?

Kate's saying: 'I'll put on too much weight if people keep bringing us goodies, then I won't be able to run away from the Mod Plods.'

Everyone laughs.

"How can you make jokes?" I ask them.

"Laughing stops you going mad," says a fair-haired, older woman called Sue.

They tell me stories about going in the base and spray-painting and it sounds really exciting. Sue says one night she got fed up with painting all the right things, like *WOMEN FOR PEACE*, and she just did *NERDY NERDY NOO NOO*.

I have to laugh, and then I see that it does make things feel better.

I ask why it's all women.

"There were men, at the start," Sue says, "but they wanted to take over. This began as a women's action, and we thought it ought to stay that way. And it shows how much we can do – we don't need men to help us."

I think of Dad – *he'd* be expecting the women to wait on him. I'm glad there aren't any men. "I've got this banner," I say.

I've made it out of an old bed sheet, with string ties.

"Can I put it up somewhere?"

"Why not?" Kate says. I tie it to a tree near the fire. It says *PLEASE CAN I HAVE A LIFE?*

The women think it's cool.

Lindsey keeps looking at me, but I've got a bigger problem than her suspicious face. The vegan soup has made me need the toilet.

They've shown me where it is, and I don't want to go there. It'll stink, and what if I fell in?

Yeah, but what else can I do?

I could go to the base and ask to use one of their nice clean American toilets.

As if.

I use the toilet-pit. I never realised fighting nuclear weapons would mean I had to crouch over a hole in the ground full of other women's poo and recycled toilet paper. I know they dig a new one every day or so; that doesn't make it any better.

It's night-time, a day later. I'm eating baked beans that I brought with me. The fire smokes so much no one will notice if I fart. I'm pickled in smoke by now; it's all through me, in my nose, my hair, my eyes.

I quite like it, actually.

Kate pulls something out of her pocket – a neat little pair of bolt-cutters. She's going into the base.

Lorna and a Dutch woman called Anneka are getting up. I get up too and whisper to Kate,

"Can I watch you go in?"

She's not sure, then she says, "Okay, but stay outside. You don't know what to do if you're arrested."

We walk along a path through the woods, and then we get to a bit of the fence that's like patchwork, it's been cut and mended so many times. Kate gets to work with the bolt-cutters; she's an expert, and soon there's a nice opening in the fence. They slide through it. Anneka's got a rolled-up thing under her elbow. I wonder what it is?

Only, I'm supposed to stay outside.

I never said I would, though. And they haven't exactly shut the fence behind them!

I push through the slit. Where have the others gone? I'm scared for a moment, but then I manage to spot one of them, a dark figure against the glare of lights from inside the base.

I go as fast and as quietly as I can, keeping behind them so they won't see me and send me back. There's a kind of bald strip along by the fence, but after that there are a lot of bushes so

I can duck down and keep out of sight. My heart's pounding.

I see mounds against the sky, and another fence round them. Rolls of barbed wire on top of the fence. Then Kate looks round and stands still. I run towards them.

"It's me. Blue."

"I knew it was you. You weren't meant to come in! Oh well."

So I can go along with them. We reach the fence.

"We've got to be quick," Kate says. "Those are the silos, where they keep the missiles."

Anneka's unrolling her bundle. It's a banner, like the one I made. It says *BREAK THE NUCLEAR CHAIN*.

Now I'm helping to tie it to the fence – that's hard because it's freezing again and my fingers are clumsy. But I feel more alive than I've ever done, even though my heart's pounding. I'm doing something to fight back at last.

"Now what?" I ask.

"*We* stay and wait to be arrested," Lorna says. "If nobody arrives, we sing. *You've* got to go back."

I want to stay with them. "I don't know the way."

"I'll take you," says Kate.

Someone's coming.

"Mod Plods," Kate says. "Run!"

I remember how the police kicked the woman when the convoy came in and I'm so scared I just take off. We're running from them, dodging the bushes – then I hear a heavy body hitting something twiggy and a lot of swearing.

"He's fallen into a gorse bush." Kate's laughing, though she's out of breath.

"There's another one coming – listen."

More running footsteps.

"This way,' she says. "I've got a hiding place…"

There are three gorse bushes that have grown round, almost in a circle. We push past the prickles and crouch down, getting our breath back.

The Mod Plods are running round, shouting, then I hear them going away again.

"Is that it?" I say to Kate. "I thought they'd come with dogs and guns."

"No – though you'd be shot if you went into the silo area. That's because we once danced on top of them and they don't want us back."

She doesn't talk for a while, then she says, "How old are you, really, Blue?"

I don't know why, I can't pretend any more. "Fourteen. Just."

"I thought you were. Why did you leave home? Apart from the nuclear stuff."

I don't answer, but she's waiting. Well, *she's* not a teacher.

"My mum died of MS in October and my dad – he just kept working and let me do all the looking after her. I was glad to, but now he thinks it's still okay for me to do all the shopping and cooking, and clean the house – I'm just his servant. He doesn't care about me any more, he hardly talks to me."

"Does he know where you are now?"

"No, he's no idea."

"He'll have the police looking for you."

I don't want to think that.

"Listen," Kate says. "I was brought up in a children's home. When I was sixteen they chucked me out, gave me a flat and left me to look after myself."

"What?"

"That's what happens to care kids. But you've got someone at home."

"No! I told you—"

"Have you told *him* how you feel?"

No, I realise, I haven't. I've just thought he *ought* to know how I felt.

"You're both grieving," she said, "and maybe he hasn't realised. And you need to go back and get your education."

"There's no point! Not if we're all going to get nuked."

"What did you put on your banner? *Please can I have a life?* You can't give up on life, or *they'll* have won. You've got to talk to your dad, tell him how you feel."

"Maybe he won't listen."

"Is there anyone who might help you talk to him?"

"There's my aunt Ruth. I like her."

"Ask her, then."

It's uncomfortable, and not just because of the gorse prickles, but I am beginning to see things differently.

"He's got to take charge of the house, and show you he loves you. I bet he does."

"He used to be nice. Before… before Mum—"

Then I'm crying, and she's holding me, and patting my back.

"Okay," I say at last.

"I know you've had a tough time," she says, "but you're lucky to have a dad. I had to be taken away from mine – don't ask why."

So I don't, but I give *her* a hug.

We're squeezing out through the slit in the fence. I say, "I so wanted to be a Greenham woman."

"You *are* a Greenham woman. You've been here, you've watched the convoy come in. You've done an action at the silos – that's no picnic. Changing things with your dad is part of being a Greenham woman. It's not just about nuclear weapons, it's about women standing up for all the things that really matter. And you can come back here, for demonstrations."

I have a thought. "I could start a CND group at school. I can think of a few kids who'd join."

The next morning, I go to a Greenham woman's house in Newbury – Lynette, she's called. She's kind, but I'm so scared.

I tell myself I've looked nuclear weapons in the face, so I can do this.

I ring my home number. Dad answers and his voice is all shaky, as if he's been crying.

I take a deep breath.

"Hello, Dad," I say.

Why I Chose the Greenham Common Women

I was deeply involved in campaigning against nuclear weapons in the 1980s. I belonged to a local peace group, but I also used to go to Greenham to demonstrate against the convoy when it came in. I regularly went in the daytime, took food to the women and fetched them wood with my car. Nuclear war did seem to be very likely in those days; it was terrifying. But going to Greenham was about more than nuclear weapons – it changed my ideas about who I was, what I could do as a woman, and what I dared think. This story is set around 1986–7, which was when I had most to do with the peace camp.

LESLIE WILSON

The Greenham Common Women Facts

Between 1949 and 1991, the Warsaw Pact countries (the Soviet Union and the Eastern European countries under its domination) and the Western North Atlantic Treaty Organisation (NATO) confronted each other with nuclear weapons. At first, it was hoped that a nuclear war would be so devastating that nobody would dare start one. This was called Mutual Assured Destruction. But in the early 1980s, the introduction of American cruise missiles and Soviet SS20s seemed to make it possible to fight what was called a 'limited' nuclear war. Exactly what that meant was always unclear, but it seemed to many that it would involve millions of dead, and might well escalate into a worldwide nuclear holocaust.

The population of the UK were issued with leaflets suggesting that they could survive a nuclear attack by going under the stairs, protected by a couple of doors and mattresses. This sparked a wave of protest from all over the country.

The women's peace camp at Greenham Common (one of the cruise missile bases) was part of this protest. The camp lasted from 1981 until 1993, and the women there survived brutal evictions and vigilante action, inspiring campaigners everywhere.

About The History Girls

The History Girls are a group of bestselling, award-winning authors of historical fiction. Some of the authors write for young adults, some for fully fledged adults and some for younger readers.

Among them, The History Girls' books cover every historical period from the Stone Age to World War II. Geographically, their novels will take readers from Trondheim to Troy, or the Caribbean to the Wild West, via Venice, Victorian England and Ancient Rome.

The History Girls blog was started by Mary Hoffman in 2011 and is a place where the authors share their thoughts on writing, research, reviews, and all aspects of their work.

the-history-girls.blogspot.co.uk

About the Authors

PENNY DOLAN

Penny Dolan works as a children's writer and storyteller, visiting children in schools, libraries and museums. She writes picture books and longer stories for children and has always been very interested in legends and history. She has studied drama and is currently working on another Victorian story. Like her most recent book, *A Boy Called M.O.U.S.E*, the new novel is partly set in the whirling backstage life of the fictional Albion Theatre. *MOUSE* was shortlisted for the Stockton Children's Book of the Year, the West Sussex Book Award and the Young Quills Award for Historical Fiction.

www.pennydolan.com

Adèle Geras

Adèle Geras was born in 1944 in Jerusalem. She was educated at Roedean School and St Hilda's College Oxford, where she read French and Spanish. She's been an actress and singer and a teacher of French but since 1976 has written full time. She's published more than 90 books for children and young adults. Her novel *Troy* was shortlisted for the Whitbread Award and Highly Commended for the Carnegie Medal. Together with Linda Newbery and Ann Turnbull, she has written two novels (*Lizzie's Wish* and *Cecily's Portrait*) for the Historical House series. *A Candle in the Dark* is for younger children and deals with the subject of the Kindertransports. She has published four novels for adults and a fifth (*Cover Your Eyes*) is due in 2014. She lives in Cambridge.

www.adelegeras.com

MARY HOFFMAN

Mary Hoffman finds that Italy and Italians often creep into her stories, as they do in her teenage Stravaganza series for Bloomsbury and her historical novels *The Falconer's Knot*, *Troubadour* and *David*. She also writes for younger children, as in her *Amazing Grace* books and the Great Big Books series with Ros Asquith. Mary has written over a hundred books and lives in a converted barn in Oxfordshire, with her husband. They have three grown-up daughters.

Mary is currently obsessed with the Tower of London and Shakespeare's theatres.

www.maryhoffman.co.uk

DIANNE HOFMEYR

Dianne Hofmeyr grew up on the southern tip of Africa and taught art and ceramics. She lives in London and writes picture books as well as young adult novels with a particular interest in Ancient Egypt and stories set in Africa. Her YA novel set in South Africa during the peace process before Nelson Mandela's release from prison won the M-Net Award. Curiosity and a love of maps and old letters have made her a writer.

Dianne's books are translated into more than 20 languages and two of her novels have been IBBY Honours books. Her latest novel is *Oliver Strange and the Ghosts of Madagascar*. Her latest picture books are *The Magic Bojabi Tree* and *Zeraffa Giraffa*.

www.diannehofmeyr.com

MARIE-LOUISE JENSEN

Marie-Louise Jensen was born in Henley-on-Thames. Her early years were largely devoted to the reading of as many books as possible. Marie-Louise studied Scandinavian and German at the UEA and has lived and worked in Denmark and Germany as well as England. She did an MA in Writing for Young People in 2005 and has been writing teen historical fiction ever since.

www.marie-louisejensen.co.uk

CATHERINE JOHNSON

Catherine Johnson would have her own outdoor heated swimming pool and at least two horses if she won the lottery. She has written books for children and young adults and also for radio, TV and film. Her latest book, *Sawbones*, was published in October 2013.

www.catherinejohnson.co.uk

KATHERINE LANGRISH

Katherine Langrish is the internationally published author of several children's fantasy novels, including the Viking trilogy *Troll Fell*, *Troll Mill* and *Troll Blood*, recommended in the School Library Association's Top 160 Books for Boys, republished in one volume as *West of the Moon*. Her fourth book, *Dark Angels* (US title *The Shadow Hunt*) was listed as one of Kirkus Reviews' Best Books for Children 2010, and the US Board on Books for Young People's Outstanding International Books 2011. Her writing is strongly influenced by folklore and legends, and has been compared with Alan Garner's.

Katherine lives in Oxfordshire and is currently writing a two-part YA dystopia. She blogs about all aspects of myth, fantasy and legends at *steelthistles. blogspot.co.uk*

www.katherinelangrish.co.uk

JOAN LENNON

Joan Lennon was born in Canada long enough ago to have experienced history first hand. She has lived in Scotland most of her adult life. She has a PhD from St Andrews University and has endeavoured, unsucessfully, to get her four sons to address her as Dr Mummy.

Her medieval series for 8–12 year olds, The Wickit Chronicles, follows the adventures of a boy called Pip with the voice of an angel and a delightful though dangerous-to-know gargoyle (technically a grotesque) called Perfect. In her Victorian series, The Slightly Jones Mysteries, also for 8–12s, her heroine's ambition is to be as great a detective as Mr Sherlock Holmes, and no baffling clues, mad scientists, Egyptian mummies or Scottish ghosts are going to stop her.

Joan is now pondering which historical period to write about next.

www.joanlennon.co.uk

SUE PURKISS

Sue Purkiss taught English in various settings before becoming a writer. She has been a Royal Literary Fund Fellow at Exeter University, helping students with their essay skills, and now fulfils the same role at Bristol University, as well as reviewing and teaching creative writing to adults. Her most recent book, *Emily's Surprising Voyage,* was long-listed for the Carnegie Medal. Set in the nineteenth century, it tells the story of two children travelling to Australia on board the first iron ship, the SS Great Britain. Her previous book, *Warrior King*, was a novel about the great Dark Age leader, Alfred the Great, and his very remarkable daughter, Aethelflaed.

www.suepurkiss.com

CELIA REES

Celia Rees has written over twenty books for teenagers, and has become a leading writer for Young Adults with an international reputation. Her books have been translated into 28 languages and she has been shortlisted for the Guardian, Whitbread and WHSmith Children's Book Awards. Her books *Witch Child, Sorceress* and *Pirates!* have won awards in the UK, USA, France and Italy. Her latest book, *This is Not Forgiveness,* a dark, contemporary thriller, has been nominated for several UK national awards and was one of Kirkus Reviews Best Teen Books of 2012 in the US.

Celia lives in Leamington Spa, Warwickshire, and divides her time between writing, talking to readers in schools and libraries, reviewing and teaching creative writing.

www.celiarees.com

KATHERINE ROBERTS

Katherine Roberts won the Branford Boase Award in 2000 for her first novel, *Song Quest*. Before becoming a published author, she trained as a mathematician at the University of Bath and wrote computer programs (which is her excuse for any spelling mistakes). Marriage took her to the Welsh border country, where she worked with racehorses while writing her first stories for fantasy and horror magazines. She currently lives beside the sea in the southwest of England, in the town where she grew up.

Katherine's books for young readers include the Pendragon Legacy quartet about King Arthur's daughter, published by Templar.

www.katherineroberts.co.uk

ANNE ROONEY

Anne Rooney can't fly planes and hasn't mysteriously crashed into the Thames – although there's a good chance she would if she tried flying a plane. She lives in a perpetual state of chaos with several chickens, a tortoise, some ferrets and some daughters.

Instead of crashing planes into estuaries, she spends her days writing both truth and lies for young people, and just the truth for adults – around 160 books in all. Each summer she spends two months teaching creative writing, which is also not dangerous.

www.annerooney.com

LESLIE WILSON

Leslie Wilson is the author of four critically acclaimed historical novels, two for adults, *Malefice* and *The Mountain of Immoderate Desires* (which won the Southern Arts Prize), and two for young adults, *Last Train from Kummersdorf* (shortlisted for the Guardian Children's Fiction Prize) and *Saving Rafael* (nominated for the Carnegie Medal, Highly Commended for the Southern Schools Book Award, shortlisted for the Lancashire Book of the Year Award and longlisted for the Wirral Paperback of the Year Award).

Leslie has lived in England, Germany and Hong Kong. She now lives in Berkshire with a husband and a dog, and has two daughters and three grandsons.

www.lesliewilson.co.uk

Now investigate the inspiring stories of
more great women in history:

Margaret of Scotland
Saint and monarch (c.1045-1093)

Gráinne O'Malley
Pirate (1530-c.1603)

Catrin of Berain
Noblewoman, 'the Mother of Wales' (1534-1591)

Queen Elizabeth I
Monarch (1533-1603)

Sarah Churchill
Advisor to Queen Anne (1590-1676)

Caroline Herschel
Astronomer (1750-1848)

Dido Belle
Aristocrat and daughter of a slave (1761-1804)

Elizabeth Fry
Prison reformer (1780-1845)

Harriet Martineau
Author, a founder of sociology (1802-1876)

Ada Lovelace
First 'computer programmer' (1815-1852)

Queen Victoria
Monarch (1819-1901)

Florence Nightingale
Founder of modern nursing (1820-1910)

Isabella Bird
Explorer and natural historian (1831-1904)

Mary Kingsley
Writer and explorer (1862-1900)

Nancy Astor
First female MP (1879-1964)

Noor Inayat Khan
World War II Allied spy (1914-1944)

Rosalind Franklin
Pioneering scientist (1920-1958)